P9-DVQ-196

Withdrawn from Collection

THE MISSING
WORD

Concita De Gregorio

THE MISSING
WORD

*Translated from the Italian
by Clarissa Botsford*

Europa
editions

Europa Editions
27 Union Square West, Suite 302
New York, NY 10003
www.europaeditions.com
info@europaeditons.com

This book is a work of fiction. Any references to historical events,
real people, or real locales are used fictitiously.

Copyright © 2015 by Giangiacomo Feltrinelli Editore, Milano
First Publication 2022 by Europa Editions

Translation by Clarissa Botsford
Original title: *Mi sa che fuori è primavera*
Translation copyright © 2022 by Europa Editions

All rights reserved, including the right of reproduction
in whole or in part in any form.

Library of Congress Cataloging in Publication Data is available
ISBN 978-1-60945-762-4

De Gregorio, Concita
The Missing Word

Art direction by Emanuele Ragnisco
instagram.com/emanueleragnisco

Cover design and image by Anna Morrison

Prepress by Grafica Punto Print – Rome

Printed in Canada

CONTENTS

THE MISSING
WORD

1.
Me About You

What did you come to tell me, Irina? Why did you come knocking at my door? "I'd like you to help me, if you can, to take the words line them up and put back together all the bits that I feel splintered and scattered throughout my body. I'd like to join the pieces, as if I were repairing a broken object, so that I can pick it up and pull it out of me. So that I can keep it beside me, carry it in my pocket, put it in my bag in one piece, one whole piece. Do you think it can be done, by writing about it? If I'd known how, I would have done it, but I didn't and I wasn't ready. Now I am. I want to put a period at the end. Mark the passage. I feel it'll be easy, if I am able to tell you everything."

So, what is the stuff of this story? and why has it bound us together for days without being able to stop and never stopping, days and days of words and laughter and tears and a voice that breaks and songs, too, have you ever heard the song that goes like this?, then love again. You, Irina, you talk about love, always.

2.
Dearest Nonna

Dearest Nonna,
I won't be there this Christmas either. I just can't be with you anymore. With Papa and Mamma, with Vittorio, and his wife and kids. I love you all terribly, you know that. I love you more than anything, and with every year that passes I realize that years are going by for you, too, I shouldn't miss a moment, I should really be there to give you a hug. But then there's that giant pink elephant in the middle of the room when we're together. The tree red candles twinkling lights children's voices singing gold-ribboned gifts. And that enormous elephant right there in the middle. That everyone pretends not to see. They circle around it in a sad do-si-do, dancing from one armchair to another without ever bumping into it, they don't touch it, they don't name it, they don't look up. Even you and I are unable to exchange glances when we're around the elephant, because our eyes are mirrors reflecting the other's pain, amplifying it, and the pain grows and grows until it is the only thing left in the room.

I know, their silence is born of the best of intentions. Looking back, I think that in this story everyone has always behaved with the best intentions: even when their actions were incomprehensible and vicious, their intention at the time was always to make things better. Isn't that awful? It's incredible how much pain we can inflict, convinced we're acting for the best. Do you see what I'm saying, Nonna? You always know everything even when you don't, you hold everything together, even things that are not meant to be held together. There's no need to explain things to you. I'm not coming at Christmas, Nonna, because when I look at Mamma and she meets my gaze, the sadness I see feels like death. I don't have the strength to deal with other people's pain. I'll take my elephant with me, I'll stroke it, ride it, dream about it. Sometimes it's pink, sometimes it's blue, and sometimes it turns into a whale in the ocean.

Dearest Nonna, I'm leaving for Patagonia with Luis next Sunday. We're going whale watching. Trekking, climbing to the top of the mountains, walking deep into the woods, sitting at the ocean shore all make me feel happy. Minuscule and at peace. Luis makes me feel happy. I'll introduce him to you one day, I'd love to. You'll like him. He has eyes that laugh and big hands. He can create silence when it's needed, then he chooses his words, picks them out, and stitches them together like embroidery. Did I tell you his job is to make cartoons for kids? They're magical. Did I tell you what he did when I rejected him at first? He gave me an incredible gift, something straight out of a film. I need to look into your sky-blue eyes to tell you, though: I want to see your shy smile while I describe the scene. It'll be wonderful.

I've been feeling so guilty about being happy again, Nonna. It's as if everyone has been saying: how can you forget, how can you leave what happened to you behind, how can you go on vacation, drink a glass of wine, love a man, find pleasure in his loving you, fall asleep afterwards. How can you still be alive, in short, and still want to be in this world? Have you forgotten the girls? Shame on you. It's as if they are saying that I'm dead, too, and that it's outrageous of me to rebel.

But I'm alive, Nonna, pain on its own doesn't kill you and I'm still alive. Hence, I have to live, because as long as I'm here, the memory of those who are no longer with us lives on. The memory, alive: alive, the girls, in my thoughts. To forget, Nonna. You've walked for a century and you know that nothing is ever forgotten and that everything should be retrievable at any moment, so that you can put it somewhere. Hold it in your hand or keep it in a pocket, set it on a bedside table as if it were a flower in a vase, go out and then come back in again and find it still there. How could we live without placating memory, which doesn't mean giving up, or forgetting, but allowing the heat to cool down, the damp to dry, everything to transform itself so that a beginning can be born from an end. So that hunger can be sated but return as hunger. So that desire can die to an ember but burn again. So that sleep can soothe your exhaustion but make you drowsy once more. Every minute of our being revolves around something that no longer exists so that something else can take place. Look. Children in nursery schools stop crying when their mothers have left, and then they run up to them laughing when they come back. Do they forget them in those hours? They can amputate your leg after an accident, like they did with Papa, and then you start walking, even driving a motorbike, with the prosthesis. Have you forgotten your leg, or is it precisely because you remember it—and at the same time, deal with its absence—that you can still move around in the world? We need to be happy, Nonna, hold our own against such inconceivable pain. We need fear in order to be brave. Absence is the true measure of presence. The gauge of its value and power.

I love you, Nonna Klara. I think of our secrets, I think back to when I used to come and see you when I was a girl, brimming with impending disasters, how you kept them at bay and covered for me, protected and guided me. I think of you as my home, my family. Everything was still to come, back then. And yet, much must still happen now. You're still there, I'm still here.

I'll be back with pictures of whales to show you, I'll tell you about the sounds they make, because whales sing, you know? I'm so sorry not to be with you for Christmas but I'm happy to be able to promise you I'll be happy. Even when I cry, which of course I will, as I do every holiday, I'll be even happier to witness the release of my tears. I'd like you to feel my joy. To try and stroke the pink elephant when everyone else snubs it, I'd like you to whisper in its ear. Tell it, Nonna, to relax. We'll lead it away from that place, we'll set it free, we'll go and see it every day but it will never be held captive again. Tell it that, Nonna. I love you. Merry Christmas.

I.

3.
ME ABOUT YOU. DOLL

You're so small, Irina. As small as a little doll. Round head round eyes round lips. Short hair, a boyish cut. A touch of lipstick, a silk scarf. You arrived here one day with your pants tucked into your boots, a big bag, out of breath—it was the stairs that did it, you soon got it back— your head cocked to the right, asking permission with a smile. You looked just like a doll. Russian, I thought, misled by your name. I'm from Ascoli Piceno, you said right away. I don't know anyone from Ascoli Piceno, I thought. What's it like? Beautiful, you said. I got married there, the photos are beautiful. This was how almost the first thing you talked about—before even saying how your trip had been, where you were traveling from, how long you would be staying— was your marriage.

You arrived and brought joy and calm into the room. I wouldn't know how else to describe it: pure joy. You appreciate everything, everything lights you up, whatever you come across is a surprise that you celebrate. The red coffee machine, the view from the window, the music on the radio—I can't believe it, I love this music so much!—an old chair, an unexpected visit. Where do you live, Irina? In Spain, right now: Southern Spain. Do you like it? I really like it, a lot. Everything's so calm, so warm, so close to Africa . . . You know, after years in Switzerland, in Lausanne,

Granada feels like a miracle. You laugh again, with your head tilted, you always laugh like that, like some children laugh. Your teeth, too, are a young girl's teeth. When you say yes, you always say it three times: yes, yes, yes. A kind of shyness, your tone dipping, a descending scale. After a while, you get attuned to it, and it turns into music, your own special counterpoint. Your Italian is polished, perfect, full of words no longer in use. The Italian of someone who learned to speak in a world of adults in the last century. I don't think you know any classroom or street language. When you were a girl, you must have looked exactly like you do now, only a little smaller, even smaller. "I lived in Brussels; I went to school there. My mother is German, my father Italian, French was the language of the outside world. I learned English well, I've worked in the United States a lot. Now I live with the Andalusians, and I'm trying to think in Spanish." All languages are yours, Irina. So, what language do you dream in? "Do you know what? I have no idea. I really don't think there's a language for dreams. Maybe mine are silent," you laugh again. "As a matter of fact, I often dream about whales, and whales don't speak."

4.
MATHIAS

Why did I marry Mathias? Not to contradict him. It didn't seem important whether we got married or not. I'd gotten pregnant, the girls were on the way. That's what I was thinking about. I said to him: if you're not ready to be with me, that's fine, you can leave. He didn't take the news of the pregnancy well. In fact, thinking about it now, I'd say it was the only time I'd seen him lose control in our whole time together. When I said I'm pregnant, he started stammering, then he cleared his throat as if he needed to cough but couldn't. He didn't want to believe it, he said no no no. How did you do it, there's no way. There's really no way, how could it have happened. It was an event he had neither planned nor predicted: inconceivable for him. Actually, I had been convinced it was impossible, too. Technically, let's say, I shouldn't have gotten pregnant at that time. And yet, it happened. I said to him: do what you want, I'm going ahead with it. He asked for more time, then he suggested a vacation together, to talk about it. We went to Egypt. We didn't talk about it, as far as I remember. Not much, anyway. He went back to being the man I knew. Calm, positive, cheerful. He had regained control of the situation. It was a good vacation, relaxed. I was happy about the pregnancy. He said: we're going to have a family so let's get married. Let's get married in Italy, at your place. I thought of home—the fields around my house, the tree where I wanted to build a wooden tree house, the one you see from my bedroom window—and I said: okay.

What was Mathias like? Physically? He was handsome. Tall, athletic, blond. Slightly cross-eyed, but I can't remember whether his eyes turned inwards or outwards. Memory plays such tricks on you: it's doing its thing all the time. It's like a circuit breaker: when necessary, it erases everything. Delete. In any case, he was cross-eyed, that I know: his eyes went in two different directions. But only slightly, it was attractive and rather hypnotic. The first time I met him, he made me laugh all evening. We were up in the mountains on one of those weekends our company would organize to get employees from different countries together. We worked for the same multinational. Me, Italian, in Lausanne; him, Swiss, in Italy. In Bologna. A kind of exchange, that's what we started talking about. There were about sixty people. He didn't strike me in any particular way, I could easily have spent the evening with others. It was just that after the presentations, he would turn up by my side. He was always there; I moved, and there he was again. Kind, polite, attentive. He told funny stories; he was always jovial. I remember he opened doors for me. An unusual gesture, old-fashioned. He was serious, a serious person. With a sunny disposition—white-blond and full of laughter—but stable. Like a rock in the middle of the sea. He insisted we should see one another again. We did. He was a man with strong, solid principles. He was very, very reliable. I don't know how better to say it: he was always there. What would later be revealed as rigidity, felt at first like confidence. He always knew what to do, how to do it, when. He had long fingers, with white half-moons on his nails. He did everything with great care. You could forget about everything because he would take care of it.

I wasn't head-over-heels in love. I was a little in love. I felt good. I lived in Lausanne, a city that was small, straightforward, calm. I had an important job as an attorney for a multinational: I traveled around the world. I used to go and visit him in Bologna, a city I loved, where I had gone to college. We would go to the cinema, a lot. In the evenings, he was the kind of man who would let you read in bed until late. There aren't many like that. I often read for hours and hours, even at night: with him, I felt free to do so. We would walk under the porticoes, eat ice cream. We'd been together for just over a year when I got pregnant. I was thirty-five, with a good job, a great salary. There are moments in life when you can't afford to get pregnant. It might be too soon, or with the wrong person. With Mathias, there was nothing wrong. I didn't feel up to making calculations about whether it was convenient or not. I thought: the baby has come, it's time, let's do it. Then I found out there were two of them. Months later. He was so calm, as always. Two or three, what difference does it make? he said. Laughing.

The first time I felt scared, and like the man by my side was a complete stranger, was one day under the porticoes in Bologna. A young boy was begging, dirty, bare-chested. It was cold. I stopped and I felt like crying. I started talking to him. He was so young. Mathias yanked my arm:

what are you doing, get away. I said: he's a kid, look. He answered: what do you care, there are millions more, let's go. I looked at his face and his light-blue eyes were empty. Bird's eyes. Sightless pits. It was a second, no more. We started walking again, and talking—I think—about the film we were on our way to see. But I was distracted by the incident, by something I'd never seen before. The total absence of compassion. Total, absolute, perfect.

Mathias has a twin brother who's identical, only grayer and more introverted. His sad alter ego. He never talked about him. He has a sister, too, who married an Italian from Rimini and then separated from him. He has a mother and a father, also separated. His mother is called Norma. I've rarely met anyone as impeccable in their stiffness. Mathias never talked about his family. Their relationship was based on facts, not emotions. Commitments, appointments, visits. I never heard them raise their voices when they were together. I never heard Mathias laugh with them, or reminisce about the past. I've never been able to imagine him as a child.

After giving birth, I got an infection: early-stage septicemia. I could have died. My mother was at my bedside, a nurse was monitoring me around the clock. Alessia and Livia couldn't stay in the room with me, of course. Mathias would come during visiting hours, in the evening. He would come into the room with his friends, who were strangers to me, and take pictures of me in bed. He introduced me: this is my wife. He didn't say my name. He said my wife. I was on a drip and I was so weak I didn't even have the strength to respond. I longed to send him away, but all I could do was turn my head the other way on the pillow. I've often thought, since, that I should have left him right there and then. I should have realized there could be no love behind that eagerness to show me off without seeing me. But part of me thought it was too late and part of me, once I got home and was feeling better, felt it would be stupid. Alessia and Livia were a miracle sent from heaven. I've never been as happy as I was with them. Nothing else mattered.

I earned more money than him. It's a horrible thing to say, but it's true. We never talked about it, and yet it was a fact: we worked for the same company and I had a higher position, I was more in demand, I traveled more, I was given greater responsibility. He felt, I think, a little frustrated, undervalued. He never said it, we never discussed the issue. But I could feel a kind of resentment in his silence. He would shut himself in his study, checking stocks and shares on his charts, he would tear pages out of the newspapers and through the walls the constant ripping sounded like little slaps.

Our house was really big, too big. There was an indoor pool in the basement that scared me. The laundry room, too, was a big square space that was always dark: I would walk past without looking inside. I didn't like it but it was beautiful, objectively speaking, and he had chosen it. Once I called a decorator to give it a fresh coat of paint. He was Italian. Mathias went around the house with a mirror to see whether he had painted the blind corners of the door frames, he climbed up ladders to check behind the wardrobes. With a mirror in his hand, yes. He said: he's

Italian, you can't trust him. We had a big argument in the car. It was Saturday, we were on our way to the swimming pool with the girls. Why did you call an Italian, he yelled, you know they're terrible workers. He stopped the car, let me out, and took off again. I didn't want to worry the girls, I just wanted him to stop yelling. I walked home. They came back four hours later. They had actually gone to the swimming pool. Alessia and Livia were rambunctious and red-cheeked: Papa bought us giant lollipops, we had so much fun, Mamma. He didn't say a word about what had happened in the car: he didn't say sorry, or anything else. As if nothing had happened.

He never raised his hand to us. His was another kind of violence. I started fearing his silences. His silent little manias. The seemingly indulgent way he undid anything I'd done and started again from scratch. He used to stick yellow Post-its everywhere: instructions. On the fridge, on the wardrobes, in the drawers. Lines of sticky notes on the bathroom mirror. The instructions—orders—were for me. I went to a domestic violence center. I didn't know who to turn to, I needed to understand how to behave in the middle of that forest of rules. They drew a picture of a spiral chute for me. They said, you are here in the center, right here. If you don't do anything, you'll fall right down to the bottom. The story always ends tragically. Get out now. That was where I first heard the expression "mental rigidity." A rigid, controlling personality. I proposed going to therapy together. He said: I'll come, but only if the therapist is German. We went. We were in couples' therapy for a while. After he'd gone missing with the girls, not one person bothered to ask the therapist for her opinion. At one point, he chose another therapist and went on his own, a couple of times with the girls. He was there the Thursday before they disappeared. The investigators didn't get in touch with her either. When I called her, she hung up on me.

For the last few months we lived together, we slept in separate beds. The house was huge, there were empty rooms. It didn't seem to be a problem. A matter of convenience, rather than anything else. I kept different hours, and I was taking care of the girls. For him, it was fine, he never objected. For me, it was a way to be able to relax at night. One of the last times we were together, I'd felt forced. I'd never experienced it, and it scared me. It was horrible. I was exhausted and he'd been anxious about a few things at work. When I said I'm moving to another room for a while, he had no complaints.

The separation was very civilized, composed. It was clear that we could not go on as a couple. It was very clear to me. Mathias was against it to begin with, but mostly because he couldn't conceive of me acting on my own initiative without taking his opinion into account. You're my wife, he said. Then, from one moment to the next, he said: fine, do what you want. Alessia and Livia were already five. Saint-Simon is a tiny village. I suggested he let the three of us stay in the family home and get an apartment for himself closer to the office: he would visit on weekends. He didn't even consider the idea of moving out of "his" house. I was the one that had to move out. To a small apartment right next to the girls' school. Mathias loved the girls, the way he looked after them was almost maternal, and they loved him back: they would have gone to the end of the world with him. After the separation, Dolores, the nanny who'd been with the girls all their life, stayed in the big house. Mathias and Dolores understood one another, they got along really well: she took care of him, too. She'd make him his favorite meals, have the clothes she knew he'd choose to wear ready for him. She was indulgent and solicitous at the same time. When Alessia and Livia came back to my place on weekdays, there were just the three of us. We didn't need anybody. Everything seemed to be working out.

For the Christmas holidays, he proposed taking the girls sailing for three weeks with some friends. It wasn't in line with our custody agreement, but the girls insisted and I said: alright, go with Papa. There are some wonderful photos from that vacation, I was pleased to know they were happy. When they returned in January, Alessia and Livia would go back to school.

We had two more weeks together.

Mathias, as always, was impeccable. The last weekend of January was his weekend with them again. He came and picked them up, then he called me on the Sunday and said: you don't need to come and get them tonight, they're fine, they're on a playdate with friends, don't worry. I'll take them to school tomorrow morning. You go and pick them up after school.

It was January 30, 2011. I never saw them again.

5.
DEAR MS. M.

To the County Clerk
Kenosha County
Wisconsin
USA

Dear Ms. M.,
I'm sorry if my insistence seems bothersome to you, but tracing the real identity of my grandmother's family is of vital importance to me. It's not a matter of curiosity, or even simply a legitimate desire to know my roots. If these were my motives, I'd understand the explanation the clerks in your office have provided in response to my application: there is no evidence that my grandmother was the biological daughter of a member of the Jeffery family; therefore, the privacy of those who are legally unrelated to me cannot be violated, even though they have been dead for many years. I have no title to the deeds, they have told me, politely but firmly.

I'd like to try and explain, if you'd be kind enough to read what follows, because I believe that, while I may have no legal right to do so, it is imperative that I trace the origins of my grandmother, Mayme Hallevi, who was born in Kenosha on October 7, 1914, taken to Italy by her father

John as a baby, and, many years later, married to Giuseppe Lucidi, my paternal grandfather.

Let me introduce myself first. My name is Irina Lucidi. I'm an attorney. I'm Italian, and my mother is German. I grew up in Belgium, and I've lived all over the world, including a long period in the United States for work. I married a Swiss-German and I've been living in Switzerland for the last few years. I'm the mother of twin girls, Alessia and Livia, who were born on October 7, 2004, exactly ninety years after my grandmother Mayme. Alessia and Livia, unfortunately, are no longer with me. They were kidnapped by their father a few years ago and I've had no news of what happened to them since. In these difficult, painful years of searching for my missing girls, in the solitude of the night, I have often seen interwoven threads, recurring dates, repeated destinies. I have remembered and put in order the few facts I've managed to gather over the years regarding the history of my grandparents and great-grandparents. No one has ever told me the whole story, but—now that I finally know it—I am writing it down here for you.

The Allevis, with no H, were originally from Visso, a small town in the Sibillini mountains. There is a spectacular and mysterious beauty about these mountains, Ms. M, I can assure you: they say the Apennine Sybil lived there, and that's where the name comes from. Ancient legend has it that she imprisoned a knight who had sought her out to discover the true identity of his parents. You see, I'm like the knight.

The Allevis were dirt poor. In the middle of the nineteenth century, one of them emigrated to Ireland looking for work and met a dancer there. They had seven children, the youngest of whom was named Giovanni, John to his mother. Not long after giving birth to her youngest—my great-grandfather—his mother, the dancer, left the family and ran away to America. John decided to go and find her when he turned fourteen. He needed to, wanted to: let's say, he decided to. He boarded a ship for the United States. I've located the documents from Ellis Island. An H was added to his surname, owing no doubt to an error in the transcription. John Hallevi made his way to Kenosha. He found work as a laborer in a bicycle factory, Gormully & Jeffery Manufacturing. Thomas Jeffery, the founder, was working on prototypes for the earliest automobiles. They were beautiful: open carriages with a motor. Four big wheels, a seat, a steering wheel. In the photographs, if you look them up, a man in a bowler hat and waistcoat smiles at the camera, full of virile vigor. Jeffery built the first Rambler; his company was sold to General Motors many years later. John went to work with him. In the meantime, he got engaged and then married an Italian girl from Kenosha called Domenica. Still today, immigrants stick together. Imagine back then. Giovanni and Domenica were both not yet twenty.

This is where the story I've put together so far gets hazy. Nobody seems to want to talk about it, even though it is perfectly straightforward. John fell in love with the factory owner's daughter. She loved him back. She may well have been married, too. A baby girl, Mayme, was born out of wedlock. The factory owner summoned my great-grandfather and made him the following offer: take the little girl, and this great wad of money for her dowry, and go back to Italy with your wife, Domenica. It must have been a lot of money. John accepted. He returned to Ascoli Piceno and bought a plot of land with the bribe. Later, he would become the biggest landowner in the region. Born poor, he ended up extremely wealthy and much-feared. When his daughter, Mayme, grew up, she married Giuseppe Lucidi, my grandfather: under Fascism, Giuseppe was made chief magistrate of the region. They had Pietro, my father.

My father remembers his grandfather John taking him in a carriage to visit the family properties. Drinking whisky first thing in the morning. Going to visit certain women in the farm workers' cottages and saying to him: Pete, wait for me here and watch the horses. Nonna Domenica, my father recounts, lived as a recluse and hardly ever went out. She could barely speak Italian. Mayme wasn't hers, but she had brought her up and loved her as if she had been, and had never had any other children. She was alone, with this one blond child, so different from her, an ocean away from her family.

Mayme's real mother, the factory owner's daughter—it was murmured on certain evenings—fell into a deep depression. She was sent to a sanatorium and was never heard from again. Not that anyone sought news of her.

Now, dear Ms. M., as you can surely understand, I can't stop thinking about this woman with no name, my real great-grandmother, whose daughter was taken away by the man she loved, never to see her again. This woman, who gave birth to a baby girl ninety years before I gave birth to my two, on the same day of the same month, and who, just like me, was robbed of her daughter by the man she had loved and still loved, the man she had trusted. I imagine her. I fantasize about her. I give her names. I see her. I feel her impotence in the face of her father's ferocious and inflexible will. I feel her hope that the dark-haired boy, that Italian called Giovanni, would refuse the devil's pact: money to take the baby away and abandon the mother, to forget her. I think about what she must have been thinking, I can think in her language, which for many years was mine. I dream about her. I imagine her disbelief when she hears that her lover and newborn child have gone, that her daughter will never see her again. I understand much better than I can explain how tempting it is to fade away to nothing. How easy it is to wish you could forget completely, but since you cannot forget a child, how attractive the idea of dying becomes. Unfortunately, pain on its own doesn't kill you. I see her, my nameless great-grandmother, in the sanatorium where her rich and powerful family had locked her up in order to eradicate her presence on the family tree. I live her days. Then my mind races to the other side of the ocean to Domenica, an Italo-American forced to move to a country that was not hers, with a daughter that was hers but not hers, to live in a remote and foreign land with a man who loved another woman without having the courage to truly love her, and who ultimately inflicted on her the punishment of his deep cowardice, his personal interest. A woman—Domenica—who never had any other children, perhaps never again shared a bed with her husband, certainly was never again loved. Finally, I think of John, the day his boss calls him in to say: here's the money, get out of here and take the baby with you, get lost. He could have refused, I think. This is the exact moment when a film script would offer a different ending: in the film, John would fling the papers off Jeffery's walnut desk, leave the room slamming the door behind him, rush to Mayme's mother and run away with her and the baby, to a new life.

But John accepted that money. He crossed the ocean and went back to Ascoli Piceno, and by Mayme, many years later, Pietro was born. By Pietro, I was born. By me, on October 7, Alessia and Livia came into this world. Just like the great-grandmother I need to find out about, I am living my life without my girls.

Everything else, Ms. M., pales in comparison against my need to know whether by chance the time we're living in does not follow a linear path but exists, rather, in an ever-present contemporaneity, where everything is in the here and now, a time frame where what has taken place, takes place, and will take place co-exist. Except that we are blind and cannot see, and in order to save ourselves, we forget, we think we are the only thing that is present and important but we are actually no more than the produce of a tree that brings forth throughout the seasons the same and different leaves, the same and different fruit. We bear the marks of the lightning bolt that struck us before we were born, we complete and replicate the design of the women and men who came before us.

As you now understand, dear Ms. M., you hold the key to my request in your hands. Since Alessia and Livia went missing, living has become infinitely more tiring for me, but also inexplicably easier. Everything is elementary now, completely clear. What we need to do is understand our place in history. These words—there are already too many—serve to remind you that you, me, and Mayme are all part of a single story, everything here today, everything now, and that a legitimate respect for a deceased person's privacy counts for very little compared to the role that fate, in this moment, has assigned you. The names of things,

Ms. M., are simply titles we give them in order to guide us through the days, towards the destiny we are the branches of: so that every single thing may appear to be a choice. My great-grandmother's name is a secret you keep and that I live in my flesh. We can pretend to choose the right thing, or surrender to the forces that give birth to us and erase us and then bring us back to life. If we don't do it, you and I, I'm sure our children will weave the threads of this pattern together. I respect the directives of your office. Whatever you decide to do—after listening to this story—will be what was supposed to be, and therefore, whatever happens, I thank you.

Best wishes,

I.

6.
DEATH NOTICE

When Mathias died, his mother published a death notice in the newspaper with my surname following his. Mathias Schepp Lucidi. It made no sense at all. Men don't take their wives' surnames anywhere in the world, as far as I know. Certainly not in Switzerland. Also, he was Swiss German and I'm Italian. He was a man, I'm a woman. I was worth much less—in their eyes—from every point of view. When we were together, before, they didn't even call me by my name: my wife, my daughter-in-law, my sister-in-law. They pointed at me and introduced me as that. A role with a possessive adjective. I never, hardly ever, heard them say: Irina. Maybe when they were telling me off. Then he killed himself, and his mother published that death notice. My Italian surname printed after his in a German newspaper.

Why did she do it? I don't understand.

What was she trying to say?

I can't explain it, I don't understand.

Dear Nonna,
Your letter made me laugh so much! I don't know anyone who still writes by hand in ink. I wouldn't know how to. And with those gothic letters they taught you at school when you were little. Altdeutsche Schrift! It's heartbreaking to imagine how long it must take you to write a letter like that, the tools you must need, what care you must take. Your wooden half-moon with blotting paper, the thought of that moves me, too. It was always on your desk, with remnants of words on the white strip: sometimes just syllables, or a capital letter, superimposed on one another, facing in different directions, some clear, others faded, an indecipherable hieroglyphic with hints of previously-thought thoughts that were still there, snagged on the paper and in the air. I used to spend hours guessing what you had written, to whom. I would conjure up people I didn't know, people from your life not mine, people you used to write to for hours in silence. Who were you writing to, Nonna?

Yes, of course I remember the mauve dress I would always ask you to show me: I was convinced it belonged to a princess. That it was yours when you were a princess, that is, alongside the king horse carriage and castle you used to tell me about, the ones you always described before going out to the opera. I remember the color of the wardrobe you kept it in, the door a little swollen as if the wood had curled like a wave, and the golden flower-leaf-shaped handles. I remember the sound it made when it opened and the smell inside. It smelled a bit like medicine and a bit like mountain herbs. It's the magic powder that keeps the fabrics beautiful, you would tell me when I pulled away from the shadowy clothes with a hand over my nose. Your wardrobe prickles my nose, Nonna, I used to say. I remember that time you picked it out just like that without even looking, your hand went in and came out holding a dress fit for brides, queens, mermaids, a dress of a color I've never seen again in any market in the Orient or store in America. You lifted it with a circular gesture of your arm and held the satin clothes-hanger up under your chin. Then you smiled that smile and made as if to dance, you behind the fairy dress, and the dress moved like it had caught in the wind.

Nonna. Of course, it would be the best present I could ask for on my birthday, the idea of having it in my house is enough to light me up, I'd hang it on the bookshelves, on the picture hooks, I'd move it from room to room so it would be constantly in view while I study or write. Do you know that I'm working on a children's film, do you remember me telling you about it? I didn't tell you that there's a boy in the story, though, a little boy with red hair who wants to become a knight, it's set in the medieval times of kings and dragons, swords and jousting, and there's a little girl, too, his companion in games and adventures, with big slanting eyes and a lock of hair that is always falling over her forehead. Beautiful as a princess, my princess. I, who have always collected fairy tales from around the world, whenever I traveled to faraway countries, who always came back with a new incredible story to show and read to my girls, do you remember how many fairy-tale books we had in every possible language? Well, now I have my own princess, my very own. I change her clothes, I give her movements, there are these huge computers in the studio and inside them there are all the drawings that fit together to make a film. They are colored and animated, they take on their own life, like in dreams.

Granada is a fantastic city. Morocco is closer than Brussels, did you know that? There's a sea breeze that blows in from another continent, you can smell Africa on it. Shall we go to Africa together one day, Nonna? Will you come with me? The young people I work with on the animations all look as though they've sprung out of a fairy tale, too. They look like the characters they draw, taken all together they're quite a sight. One boy is tall and thin, another one is short and fat, one girl has black curly hair and pointy shoes, another one is as thin as a rake and wears boots that stretch up over her knees. They're always laughing, always talking, they drink coffee at all times of day and eat cinnamon buns incessantly, just like kids. Luis is one of them.

I know, I told you I'd talk about it when I saw you, but too much time has passed and I feel like new memories are pushing the old ones back, I'm scared that when we meet, I'll have so many things to tell you that I won't be able to find the right words for each and every one of them. Words sometimes create a flood, other times they dry up. Or they come too late and are no longer useful to express what they wanted to say. Words are precise mechanisms. In your language, in the language we shared when I was a child, they are perfect interlocking building blocks. But words have their own rhythm, it's vital to find them at the right time. In short, what I want to tell you now is just this one thing.

I met Luis by chance, in Indonesia, when the guide I'd asked to accompany me one day to a certain village—I was going to visit a school I'd heard a lot about, a children's center—said: yes, I can come with you this afternoon. If you don't mind, however, there'll be two Spaniards coming too. If you don't mind. Do you see, for example, how the word "mind" changes when you've been through so much? I don't mind anything, Nonna. I really don't mind anything any longer. Everything feels like a surprise and a gift. When I hear people around me who get upset about trivial little things I think, watch out, let the sleeping dragon lie: it may wake up one day. If I'm overtired, or overwhelmed by the missing voices and faces, then I simply don't notice what's going on around me. So, no, I don't mind anything, ever.

Luis and his traveling companion, a friend, knew nothing about me, nor did I know anything about them, of course. Chance traveling companions. I can hardly remember the journey to the village. Luis must have been sitting behind me: if I make the effort to remember that day it's as if I can feel the shadow of a presence in the seat behind mine. I gazed out of the window, and talked only to the guide. The children in the school were wonderful, Nonna. Barefoot, in class, at their mismatched desks. They knew a few words of English, I told them some stories and drew a few pictures, they showed me theirs. I kept two of them. They're here on my desk, now. Six-year-old kids, like our girls.

The following day, I was back in the city. I went into a post office to mail some letters and send a few things home. It seems unlikely in a city as big as that, as crowded with people running around, as noisy and distracted, but this is what happened: we bumped into one another at the entrance to the post office. I was on my way in and he was leaving. He recognized me; I wouldn't have recognized him. What a surprise, he said. And straight after, on an impulse: why don't we have dinner together tonight? We only have one more day to go, tomorrow we're catching a plane home. It's our last night, it would be nice to celebrate meeting like this.

Luis's English was so incomprehensible, his accent so strange, that I asked him to speak Spanish to me instead. I couldn't understand everything he said, but I caught the gist. Spanish is beautiful. Luis and his friend had a way of saying things that made them sound like lyrics, a song they knew by heart. She started a sentence and he finished, or vice versa. Both of them, as if it were the chorus, would repeat: todo cuadra. What does todo cuadra mean? I asked them in slow English. Everything adds up. Todo cuadra, Nonna, means that in the end everything ends up in its place. Luis says it a lot. As often as I say: really? As often as you say: okay? He says it even when it doesn't seem to have anything to do with the conversation, but in the end it always does. Todo cuadra.

We exchanged emails, we started corresponding. My solitary journey went on for several weeks, he went back to

Spain. Every now and again, when I was able to get an Internet connection, I'd check my email and find his letters. I imagine he must have looked me up on the Internet, he must have found the newspaper articles, someone must have told him my story. It wasn't me, in any case. We never talked about it in our emails. Our letters were long and beautiful. I could be just Irina in them, I went back to being Irina and nothing else. I told him about the things I saw, described places, my thoughts, we recommended music and books to read to one another. We never said a thing about the facts. He never asked me. That, Nonna, was when I felt as though life might belong to me again one day. Because, as you know, it hasn't belonged to me for many years, I haven't been myself for many years. After Alessia and Livia went missing, I, too, simply disappeared.

When I came back to Europe, he asked if we could meet again. He invited me to Granada, his city. After all, we'd only ever spent one evening together, he said. Apart from the journey to the village, of course, but on that trip, he'd only seen the back of my neck. Every email made me laugh. I said: no, Luis. I don't want to see you again. I don't want to see anyone. I can't, I'm not interested, I don't have the strength or the desire. Really, don't be offended. There's no room inside me for anyone: all the space is taken. Forgive me, but no. Let's keep writing, if you want.

A few weeks later, I was due to give a presentation for the foundation Missing Children Switzerland in Brussels. A public ceremony, which was really important: we were being recognized as part of a European network. We would be linked to sister associations throughout Europe. The searches, support, all our work for missing children and their families would be given renewed impetus.

I was behind the dais on a raised platform in the conference room. I was speaking to the audience, the room was small but very crowded and warm. I didn't see Luis until the end: leaning against the doorframe at the back of the room. He'd come from Granada without telling me. He'd looked up the time and place of the conference, taken a flight, and come to listen. When we'd finished speaking, the other members of the association and I were surrounded by people handing out their cards, with stories to tell. We were still seated, with throngs of people standing around us, kind, interested people. Each of them deserved my full attention. Then I heard his deep voice. His face a few centimeters from mine. He said: I came to bring you a birthday present. He put a small cloth pouch into my hands, smiled, and left.

There was a set of keys, Nonna, in the pouch tied with a drawstring. Keys, a card with an address, and this: *These are the keys to my home. It's yours, too. You can use them when you want, or never. They are your keys. Todo cuadra, love.*

Many months passed before I was able to allow myself to meet him. Not at his house, of course. In Amsterdam. I have to go for the foundation, I told him: if you want, we can meet there. It was really nice in Amsterdam. With him, I was just Irina once again. We never talked about the facts, ever. We carried them around with us without mentioning them. Luis has two adult children from a failed marriage. He knows about marriages, children. He knows about pain. When I walked into his house in Granada the first time, much later on, he showed me around the rooms. When we got to the children's rooms upstairs, he said: this is L's room, this is F's. But when the girls come back, L and F will share one room and the twins will share the other. Just like that, as if it were a simple fact. As if it were a possibility. They won't be coming back, Nonna, I know. But I couldn't live without knowing there's a place for them in my home. A place waiting for them, if they were ever to knock and say: where are we sleeping in this house, Mamma?

The birthday with the keys was two years ago. The idea that you want to mail me your princess dress for the next one makes me feel sixteen again. But in a few days, I'll be forty-eight, Nonna. And I'm not as beautiful as you were at twenty, when you must have looked like a cloud of lilac at parties. I'm not as tall as you, nor am I blond, I can't tie my hair up in that bun which, seen from behind, looked like a volcano of whipped cream, nor do my eyes match the dress. That was why you chose it, wasn't it? Because it was the same color as your eyes. I've only just realized, now I know. Only you, Nonna Klara, can be a princess at that party. But I promise that I'll try it on just once, in secret. I'll stand on a stool so that the dress will fall to the ground and cover it, then I'll take a picture in the mirror and send it to you by email. You've learned how to open email attachments, haven't you, Nonna? Remember how to do it, I explained it to you: put the cursor on the paper-clip icon and click twice. Of course you know how to do it, sorry. I'll wear a hat, too, if I can find one that goes well with that color. That way, I'll be able to hide my short, boyish haircut. A raffia hat, there are lots of them here in Granada, with a flower. One day, sooner or later, I'll grow my hair out again, Nonna. Like when I was little. When it's grown down to my shoulders, I'll come and ring at your door. It'll be my gift for your hundred years, which are just a handful and feel like a short breath. Let's make a pact, do you want to share a secret with me?

You're a wonder of life, Nonna.

Ich liebe dich. Te quiero con locura.

8.
ME ABOUT YOU. WHALES.

So that's how you told me about Alessia and Livia, your daughters, talking about whales, with no preface. "I've always dreamt about water, about the world underwater. Then, one day, when Alessia and Livia were no longer there, I dreamt I was in a kind of city made of dark wood, built on stilts, in the middle of the sea. A floating city. At the center of the blocks of buildings, in a kind of inner-sea courtyard, there were two little whales playing. They chased each other, puffing out great jets of water, they bumped noses then disappeared underwater before resurfacing suddenly, playing hide and seek. The sound they made was reedy, like laughter. They lived there. They were the baby whales of the city. I'm sure of it."

9.
Dear Dr. S.

Dear Dr. S.,

I fear you will disapprove of my decision to write to you because, as you've told us many times, the point of the couples' therapy Mathias and I are undergoing with your guidance is that every issue should be shared. That we tell one another, in fact, in your presence, what we dislike and what bothers us so that, by talking about it together, we succeed in untangling the issue. To speak without any inhibitions, that's what you invite us to do: don't leave anything outside the room.

However, after our last two meetings this week, I came out with a terrible feeling of injustice, I would even say of exclusion. I had the feeling, Dr. S., that you and my husband have developed a tacit agreement that our situation is somehow my fault. As if Mathias is the victim of my decision to seek a separation, as if my decision is not necessarily a whim, but a deplorable though legitimate act of willfulness. I know it can't be true, that you don't judge, and would never take one side over another. But this is what I feel and—in accordance with your advice—I think I need to express it. I would find it hard to say it in front of Mathias: I'm scared I would embarrass you and put you on the defensive. I'm scared my husband would end up protecting you, and that this would simply make the suspicion I'm telling you about even worse. This is why, after thinking about it a great deal, I've decided to write to you tonight in private.

Dr. S., I'd like to talk to you again about the matter of the Post-its. I felt like you were dismissing my concern as capriciousness, I even thought I could see the shadow of a smile on your lips. You hardly let me finish my account, while Mathias was shaking his head all the way through. You said: Yes, but apart from the sticky-note instructions on how to lock the door, is there anything else we'd like to talk about now? Meaning, something more relevant.

No, there's nothing more relevant for me right now. I don't know what your house is like, Dr. S., nor who you live with, and I can't—of course—ask you. But I have wondered how you would react if you opened your eyes in the morning and found a sticky note on your bedside lamp instructing you how to turn the bathroom light on: *first close the door, then turn the light on.* If, going downstairs to the kitchen to get breakfast for the girls, you found another note indicating how much cereal to pour into the bowls, what type of milk to use, and at what temperature. I wonder whether you really would find it amusing, quirky, perfectly reasonable. You may. I might be too sensitive. But let me explain.

The first time I found a minutely detailed list of the clothes they were supposed to put on stuck to Alessia and Livia's wardrobe, in two columns side-by-side under their names in capital letters, I thought it was attentiveness and it made me smile, too. Mathias can't stand when the girls are dressed alike, and in perfect agreement we've never done so, but there were times when we were in a hurry to get dressed for school and they might have ended up with—I don't know—the same socks, say. Socks all look the same anyway, you're not exactly going to be checking whether they put on the ones with balloons or the ones with daisies. Sometimes you buy them in packs and some of them are the same, sometimes the ones you're looking for have been put in the wash and you pull out another pair without looking. In short, it happened occasionally. So, the first time I found the list, I simply followed the instructions, which included the order in which the clothes should be put on—first, their vests, of course, stripes for Livia, plain for Alessia, then their long-sleeved tops, one green, one yellow, then their blouses on top, different ones. In the days and weeks that followed, the sticky notes started to multiply. Sometimes, when the instructions were too long to fit on the Post-it, there were sheets of printing paper stuck—for example, on the fridge—with tape: *the milk must be warmed in the milk pan not in the microwave, it must be poured after the cereal has been put in the bowl, not before.* Things like that. Things I'd always done without thinking. One day, however, I suddenly saw them as written instructions. They soon became orders: from invitations to imperatives. Not *Keep closed* but *Close!* These details, these little domestic affairs, can easily be put on the back burner in family life. When you're in a hurry, or you're hesitant to start a pointless argument, when you think that in the end it's just the other person's weakness, certainly when you feel you're the stronger of the two, you humor them, somehow you understand them, ultimately you tolerate them. In a certain sense, it's an act of arrogance. I can't deny that I was never in that state of mind: that I never felt more solid than him, more able to tolerate him, indulge him.

Then one afternoon, Elizabeth's mother came over to pick up her daughter and stayed for a cup of tea. She asked me, smiling: have you found a new babysitter? She was looking at the instructions stuck on every cupboard door, there was even one behind the front door: *when you come in, turn the key once or three times, an odd number at all times, and leave the key in the lock.* Have you found a new babysitter, she asked. And so, through the eyes of that person, who was neither a stranger nor a friend, I saw clearly what we had come to. No, we hadn't found a new babysitter. Those meticulous instructions were addressed to me. Instructions as to how to behave with Alessia and Livia, how to keep them safe—how to avoid risk—in the house. How to barricade ourselves inside the house, I would now say. They were all correct, don't misunderstand me. Perfectly sensible recommendations. But, Dr. S., I'm asking you now: accepting the fact that the person you live with suffers from an anxiety disorder, as you call it, and that it's possible to understand and tolerate their need to control how every single action, even the most natural, should occur, well, I'm asking you, how would you feel if, moving around your house, day by day, you found yourself surrounded by sticky notes that order you to behave as you already behave? Would you simply get used to it in silence? If, in addition, the person who wrote the notes were there, right beside you, would you find it normal that, instead of speaking to you, or telling you once and for all something like, always turn the key three times, it's safer, they decided not to say a word and write it on a Post-it instead, festooning the whole house with protocols and instructions?

Because, you see, Dr. S., it may sound like a bizarre

detail. If you told a friend about it, you'd probably feel an obligation to minimize it, to smile like you did last Thursday. That's what I did with Elizabeth's mother, in fact. I smiled. I said: No, no, it's one of Mathias's things, it's his way. How strange, what a weird mania. Each to their own, after all. We don't want to shame people's intimate weaknesses, do we? Marriage is a pact sealed by reciprocal needs. But I can assure you, I feel a great weight on my chest when I'm making toast for the girls' snack and I read on the wall how many minutes I'm supposed to leave the slices in the toaster, and it doesn't make me want to laugh. It makes me feel useless, incompetent, foolish. It makes me feel even more controlled than I did when I was a little girl and my father would say to me: I told you that's the wrong sweater, now do me a favor, go back to your room and get changed. A wave of anger washes over me, Dr. S., and a longing to escape that I think we should talk about in your therapy room. So, I hope you don't consider this letter too inappropriate. In the end, I just wanted to ask you if we could possibly examine together in our next session—if you brought it up, I'd be grateful, it would help me with Mathias—the matter of the Post-its.

With cordial and renewed trust.

10.
DOLORES

I can't remember precisely when I first met Dolores. I should be able to, I know. Some mothers spend months casting around for a babysitter. Interviews, trial periods. I remember another mother who used to work with me. It took her two years: she talked about nothing else, there wasn't a thing about any of them that she accepted. It had become an obsession; even at the coffee machine, it was all she talked about to whomever came along. How to find the right person. It made me laugh. Right for who, in any case? Right for her, I thought. Right for assuaging her guilt, therefore impossible to find. Kids adapt. Our childhood, mine and my brother's, was easy and chaotic at the same time. I don't think our parents ever spent much time thinking about who would look after us. A grandmother, a babysitter, a friend. They lived their lives and we spent a lot of time on our own. We weren't the ones to dictate how our days would be spent. On the contrary, I would spend whole afternoons sitting on the sofa while my grandmother read opera librettos to me. We were the ones who adapted to the rhythm of the adults, to their tastes and habits. Not the other way around. I remember that my first impression of Dolores was that she was mature, maternal, and straightforward. She was the first person I'd interviewed for the job. I was very happy. I was pregnant with twins and I was happy. I offered her the job, she gratefully accepted.

She had come recommended by the concierge at the apartment building in Lausanne where I used to live. I'd asked whether she knew anyone who would be willing to come to Italy for a while. Mathias was working in Bologna and I was planning to spend at least the first few months after giving birth with him. The concierge knew a woman who was looking for work. She was Spanish, she told me. She would be willing, happy even, to travel.

Dolores was from La Coruña, where Spain meets the ocean. All there was on the horizon was the sea, and beyond that, South America. She was the eldest of eight siblings from a very poor family, she'd married a Portuguese man when she was very young and emigrated with him to Belgium. Her life got worse rather than better. She'd already left one foreign country behind. She must have had a very unhappy life. She spoke very little. I couldn't tell you how old she was, I can't remember. "Stuff" from before I hardly remember any more. It's not true that oblivion doesn't exist. Your mind sifts, constantly storing and discarding. It creates space, wipes things out. Maybe it doesn't eliminate every trace, but it compresses them into an illegible format. Even if you really try, you can't find the key, you can no longer decipher it.

Fifty-five, perhaps. Between fifty and sixty. She was very maternal with Alessia and Livia. There was nothing they needed that she hadn't already thought of, prepared, predicted. She came to the house early in the morning and stayed until six in the evening. I took the girls to school at eight, she went to pick them up after lunch. Mathias usually came home in the early afternoon. I traveled a lot. At that time, I oversaw my company's activity in Asia. I would be away for short periods often, or longer periods rarely, a few days a month or a few weeks a quarter. When I was away, Dolores and Mathias had dinner together after putting Alessia and Livia to bed, sometimes she stayed the night. She had her own room. She had a special understanding with Mathias. They laughed a lot. She looked after him in a way he would have liked me to, I imagine. Or as he would have liked his mother to have done, if it is possible for a child to want something he doesn't know. In any case, Dolores was perfect for them. I've never been jealous, I don't know what jealousy is. I saw that Alessia and Livia were so attached to her that her name was on their lips all the time. In their needs, in their stories. I wasn't jealous, no. Love multiplies, it doesn't divide.

Every now and again, I could hear disapproval in people's voices about my being absent, being away for my work. In the small village where we lived, and in Switzerland in general, women with children tend to stay at home. Women weren't allowed to vote until the seventies in Switzerland. The day before yesterday, practically. The country is very, very sexist. Mathias never made me feel bad about going away. But with Dolores he had a secret, encrypted complicity. I could sometimes see, in the little details, that they were in agreement about this, too: she has to go, they would say to one another. She. It felt a bit like they both thought they were doing my job for me. Without saying so, though. Or rather, without saying it out loud.

No, I don't think they had a different relationship from the one I witnessed. She was much older than him. But who knows? The ties that bind people, the shared needs that lock into place, are mysterious alchemies. When they were on their own, they behaved as though they were Alessia and Livia's real parents. Then, without fail, as soon as I got home, Dolores withdrew. She quietly slipped back home. We never spent that much time together, she and I. In fact, almost none.

Mathias left her some money in his will. He thought of her that Sunday, or the Saturday when he wrote it, I don't know. I'm almost certain that the previous Saturday the handwritten will was not in the drawer. I'm convinced he left it there that last weekend. If, on the other hand, he'd had it ready and kept it hidden, it would mean he'd been planning what he then went and did all the way along, but that can't be true. I don't think it's conceivable that he was thinking of killing himself when he left for his Christmas vacation in December. A vacation with friends, three weeks on a yacht. I don't believe it for one minute. He wrote the will afterwards, when he got back.

Probably after we'd had that argument about the divorce. Anyway. One paragraph of his one-page last will and testament was for Dolores. After all, he was very grateful to her, I understand that. He had dinner with her Saturday evening, before taking off.

No, I really can't understand why, in the days between Sunday, when Mathias took off in our car, and Thursday, when he killed himself, those five days when we knew nothing about Alessia and Livia, Dolores didn't feel the need to help search for them, to come with me to the police, to give a statement about their last encounter. I don't understand why she went missing, why she, too, vanished into thin air. She'd brought them up day after day for six years. Their whole life. She'd lived in our house. She was almost like a mother to them. What I can't understand is her absence in that moment of fear.

I was scared from the start. Of course I was. When I walked into the dark, empty house and found their stuffed toys and pajamas on their beds. The girls' car seats were in the other car at my place. Mathias would never have taken Alessia and Livia in the car without strapping them into their car seats in the back. Never ever. It was an article of faith. My heart leapt into my throat. I called Dolores right away, she was the first person I called. Where are Alessia and Livia? I don't know, ma'am, was all she said. I don't know. Three days went by before she came over to the house. Monday, Tuesday, Wednesday. We had no news of Mathias. The police were looking for him. She came to see me with a friend, they stayed a few minutes in the sitting room, then they left. As if it were a courtesy visit, a formal gesture.

I haven't heard from her since. I know she went to Mathias's funeral, I know she sees his mother, his siblings. But I have never seen her again. She never answered my letter.

11.
LIST. ANGER

Things that still make me angry (getting to grips with them, dismantling them, not obsessing).

1. When, on the third anniversary of their disappearance, in an editorial meeting at that Swiss newspaper, someone suggests: "What about going back to the Lucidi case? Let's check how the search for Alessia and Livia is getting on," and then someone else, a managing editor, a woman, says, "No, not the Lucidi case again. No way. It's been covered enough, it's old news. Nobody's interested. Let's think of something else." Questions: how does a journalist get to decide that two little girls who vanished into thin air are "old news"? Old for whom? It's been covered enough on the basis of what criteria? Is there a time limit for talking about an unsolved case? If there is, what is it? Very important to know. One year? Two years? Especially a woman: what motivates a woman with such great responsibility to determine that another woman who is looking for her missing children—the Lucidi case—is not interesting? (Picture her. Try and understand what irritates her. How she spends her time. Imagine that she might have a terribly painful secret that this

painful story brings back. Idea: she's defending herself, not attacking. Understand. Don't give resentment
any space.)

2. When the reporter goes to the police chief of the Swiss
    canton and asks how the investigation is going and the
    police chief answers: "Investigation? What investiga-
    tion? Have you read the email Mrs. Lucidi sent to her
    husband? There's little to investigate. It's pretty clear."
    (Reread the email as if somebody else sent it. Identify
    things that may offend: there may be some. Imagine
    the quality and quantity of the work the police chief has
    to do: maybe there are more important and more seri-
    ous things that occupy his attention? Imagine his life,
    the women in his life. Mother? Wife? Daughter(s)?)

3. When the policeman, the evening the girls went miss-
    ing, answers: "It'll be okay, ma'am. Your husband is
    Swiss German, not Brazilian. He'll be back."
    Brazilian? Really? Brazilian? (Look for biographies of
    remarkable Brazilians. Idea: a Brazilian vacation trip.
    Study Portuguese. Download Brazilian music. Caetano
    Veloso.)

4. When the couples' therapist hangs up on me saying,
    don't disturb me again. (Hard. Ask for an opinion
    from someone who knows about professional conduct.
    Try and imagine there's a protocol. Talk to Luis about
    it at some point. There may be a problem with the
    phone, causing it to hang up on its own. Rejection,
    exclusion, infancy. Hard.)

5. When his therapist sends you an invoice for their last two sessions in order to settle the bill with a note inside saying: *Given the circumstances, I'm forwarding this to you.* (Given-the-circumstances. Imagine: how long she took to find the right formula, in her view. Not too long, spontaneous? A long time, did she think about it at length? Pity her, whatever the case.)

6. When I find out that the police have not sealed our house, that Mathias's boots are still there, full of mud. When I go to the police with his muddied trekking boots and tell them: our neighbors saw him wearing these on Sunday morning, before he went missing. Where did he go, why did he change them, why did he leave them at home? Why don't they analyze the earth in the treads, which might yield something for our search? The police answer: Ma'am, all earth is the same, all woods are the same. (Woods, the same. Earth, the same. No, they are certainly not, but think yes, in a certain sense, they are. In another sense. The earth is the same, from inside. From very close up. From very far away. The same. From the stars. Earth. Water. Air.)

7. My mother-in-law's death notice with my surname following Mathias's. (My mother-in-law. Don't use "my." Mother-in-law. Person. Mother. Norma. Unhappiness. Don't go there.)

12.
DEAR MATHIAS

To Mathias, by email
January 26, 2011

D ear Mathias,
I was really pleased to hear from Alessia and Livia that your sailing trip went so well. I hope the vacation brought everyone a little serenity. The vacation was very long, in fact. Longer than stipulated in our agreement: three weeks without the girls was hard for me, but when they're happy, I'm happy.

Now that we're going back to our winter routine, I wanted to go through a few little matters with you. Marginal things, but still important. All the traffic fines come to me, as the car is registered in my name. Since you're the one driving it, and I'm planning to let you keep it, I'd like you to sign the official change of ownership papers and put the insurance in your name. It's a little annoyance, but you need to do it.

I can also see from our bank statements that you're using our shared bank account for your personal expenses. That was not what was agreed upon. Our shared account is for Alessia and Livia's upkeep, meaning, of course, the shopping—food, clothes, school materials, sports equipment—and any other expenses, even unexpected ones, for the two of them during the periods they're with you. When they're with me, I use my personal account, as you know. Therefore, I don't want you spending the money in our shared account on your trips, your restaurants, or your taxes. Please use your own account for these expenses.

Finally, Mathias. No, I have no intention of moving back in with you in the new year because "you're very sad," as you told Alessia and Livia to convey to me. I beg you not to use the girls as go-betweens for messages, not to entrust them with requests or entreaties, not to manipulate them in the hope that their supplications will obtain something that you and I have already deemed impossible. It's cruel towards the girls. Don't be cruel with them. We can discuss what there is to discuss between adults, let's protect them for as long as possible.

While we are on the subject, in the upcoming weeks we need to file the divorce papers. Mine are ready, and I'm confirming here my determination to proceed. I would like you to get yours ready, too, so that when we are summoned by the magistrate there are no delays owing to any noncompliance on your part. I know you are extremely exacting and thorough. Try and be the same in these circumstances, which are hard for everyone.

Thank you. Let's be in touch about school times on Friday.

I.

13.
Dear Paola

Dear Paola,

The two days of our weekend won't be enough to tell you about my wonderful trip to Patagonia. I can't wait to come to Rome and stay with you. Only forty-two days left, I've been crossing them off my calendar since we decided on the date. Luis laughs every morning at breakfast when I cross out the boxes. He says that when he was a kid, he used to open a little window every day counting down to Christmas, he knows it's a serious business. You'll come to Granada one day, won't you, to see the studios where we make cartoons, our house, our friends? Will you come and stay a little while with me and Luis? Because you need to see it, no stories can live up to it. I've been feeling so refreshed since I've been here: refreshed and a little girlish, like many years ago, I feel like Irina again. Like me, that's all. Just me.

But you know this.

Every now and again, I think: how lucky I am to have always had you close, what a wonderful friendship we have. You, who can always laugh, who can see the wider angle, point it out and talk about it out loud, have a sense of humor about it. If you hadn't been there when I couldn't go out because the TV trucks were camped out and crowds of journalists were crammed outside my door. Months, do you remember? I would say, every morning: well, they must have gone. Today, you'll see, they'll have grown tired of us. What are they waiting for, at the end of the day? What do they want? But no, they were still there, and that's when you came along. Every time with a bottle, with a story about something amazing that had happened at work, with an imitation of some kind. Then you would say: come on, let's get out across the rooftops. We tried once, do you remember when I got stuck in the skylight? I was so scared, I laughed till I cried. Then I sometimes saw you crying, and I had to be the one to say, it's okay, please stop, it's okay. You'll see, we'll make it. And you'd say: Make what? A cure for this conjunctivitis? Of course we'll make it.

You're great, Paola. I have to thank you by letter because you wouldn't let me do it in person. I love that you went on an Ayurveda diet with me when I decided I had to purify my body with white rice, water, and herbal teas for weeks on end. I love that you arrived with a spicy chicken dish one evening. I love that you hunted down all the Brian Weiss books for me, when I was in my hypnosis phase, and that you helped me answer all the letters from fortune-tellers and psychics, when ten or more of them poured in every day. That you drew a map so that you could mark every spot where they had "felt" Alessia and Livia's presence: in Mexico, South Africa, Russia, in the sea, in Corsica, in Italy, in the Ukraine, in Jamaica. That you showed it to me one day, without saying a word. A map of the world constellated with penned-in circles and stars. We carried on, that time. Astrologers, cabals, triangles were added. We were one step away from the shamans. Then you said: you see, they're seeking you out.

They need you. It's true, that's it, you were right. It's awful to say, but there was a moment when I felt as though they were having fun. A macabre sort of pleasure, of course. Every one of them, along with the members of the public listening with their hands clapped to their mouths and begging for more.

I love that you kept my adorable parents at a suitable distance, on some of those days, and that you managed to teach me a few tricks on the computer, so that we were able to find some really unusual music that I'd heard once and that was so amazing I absolutely had to listen to it again. I love that you were happy, I could see it in your gaze, when I told you I'd decided to go and visit Luis in Granada, in the house whose keys had been in my possession for a good while already. You were truly happy, you almost jumped for joy.

You've never said never to me, but how could you? You've never thought it. There's no trace of hypocrisy, pretense, or theatrics in the way you are with me inside my story. It is what it is. It is this, the whole thing. It's as if there were no before or after for you. As if I've always been me, in your eyes: me laughing and crying, me and no one else. By the same token, you are still Paola. Identical.

If I had to explain what a friend is, I'd say this. A friend is a person for whom nothing changes even when everything has changed.

Forty-two days. Nearly there. I'm bringing you a present from the Tierra del Fuego that will make you blush with embarrassment. You wanna bet? When I saw it, I said: it's hers, whatever it takes. Luis said: you do the bargaining, I don't want to be involved. He was laughing.

Kisses, Paoletta, I can't wait.

PS. Yes, book the tickets for the concert. Then, if at the last minute we don't want to go, we can go to the box office and give them to a couple of kids we like the look of, like we did that time in Geneva. Kiss you.

14.
LIST. HAPPINESS

What makes me happy

1. Update this list at least once a month. Erase things (not many), change them (sometimes), add things (when I can).
2. The dialogue in *Casablanca*.
3. Sea water. The sea.
4. Pippi Longstocking.
5. Schubert's *Die Winterreise*.
6. Whales. Las ballenas jorobadas. Humpback whales.
7. Treehouses.
8. The Sierra Nevada.
9. Luis.
10. Kids' books, when they are beautiful (almost all of them).
11. Red wine, when it's good.
12. Mountain walking, uphill. Movement. A breeze on me.
13. Some words. Some idiomatic expressions like "rempamplin-flan" which means don't pay it any mind, apparently.
14. Woods when the light just filters through the trees.
15. Children's scribbles on adults' paper, and even on their walls.

16. My Nonna.
14. Going to the movies.
18. Compassion and modesty. Together, even better.
19. Vera, David's mother.
20. Dreaming about Alessia and Livia forever.
21. Luis's voice, even without Luis.
22. Making someone happy.
23. Smiling at a stranger on the street and seeing what effect it has.
24. Discovering nice music that I didn't know.
25. Sleeping when I'm tired. Sleeping through the night.
26. Writing, reading. Writing about what I've read to friends.
27. Friends.
28. An unexpected kiss, when you don't see it coming and it almost scares you, to begin with.
29. Listening to someone who is indignant and right to be.
30. Riding a racing bike, flying.
31. Working on a project with someone. Achieving, together.
32. Louise Bourgeois with a sculpture under her arm. That photo, that sculpture.

15.
ME ABOUT YOU. THE FACTS ARE SIMPLE

The facts are simple, horrific, and well-known. One Sunday in January 2011, the last of the month, your husband Mathias went to pick up the girls—your beautiful blond daughters, just turned six, twins but different, one plump one skinny—from a neighbor's house where they'd been on a playdate. You'd been through a separation, that weekend the girls were with him. At roughly 1 P.M. he looked out over the garden of the house where he'd sent them on a playdate and called out to them. They, the neighbors, said, hurry, girls, Papa is calling you: go now, it's time for lunch. Alessia and Livia ran home. They haven't been seen since. He drove off at around four that afternoon. In your car. Were they with him? Weren't they? The car seats were with you. You found the soft toys the girls would never go to sleep without in their place on their beds. Mathias went on a long journey, from Saint-Simon, the village near Lausanne where you lived, across France and then to Corsica by ferry and, again by ship, to Cerignola in Puglia. He parked the car carefully, went into the station, stood on the platform and waited for a train to come. He threw himself under the train. That's how he killed himself. At some point during those five days, he wrote a message for you: "The girls didn't suffer, you'll never see them again." No trace of Alessia or Livia has ever been found.

16.
YOUR HONOR

Your Honor,
There are no words to express my gratitude to you for receiving me. On a Saturday, moreover, your day off, opening the doors to your office yourself with your own keys in that giant, empty building. I was moved to see you arriving on your own, parking your little car in the empty lot, and coming towards me with a smile. Please forgive me if I am being too familiar, but I know solitude and appreciate it, it's not my enemy, it's the opposite: over time, it has become both a companion and an ally. I say over time, because at the start it was like a war. Absence besieged me, like an army would a fortified citadel. It rained arrows and cannonballs on me, waiting for night-fall, exploiting my weaknesses, seeking them out in order to conquer me. It wore me down with the waiting, because, you know, Your Honor, waiting for your loved ones is not a parenthesis; it's a monstrously tiring, never-ending occupation, a battle against your worst possible thoughts. It's a space that fills with monsters and creeps up on you from behind. Years go by, minutes stand still. Time flies, but every passing moment reminds you that you would rather have spent, or should have spent, that very same moment with your loved ones, them and only them, because no one else will ever be the same, and so, why

aren't they there? Why would the same people who endow your life with strength and light by dint of their very existence, to whom you would entrust your entire life, do that to you? If they're not here, where else could they be, and why? Why? This is the question that no book, no place, no drug, no psychic can appease.

Forgive me, I'm losing my thread. I just meant to say that in those few steps you took towards me, I saw solitude in you, and that now that I know how powerful and beautiful it can be, I would have liked to say to you: hello, here I am, welcome.

You asked me, as soon as we met, to give you the facts. That's the right approach. Facts. Whenever I list them out loud, I'm amazed by how many gaps and unknowns there are in the investigation. Despite your self-control, I could see that you yourself couldn't believe the number of oversights and mistakes that had been made. It was a Swiss investigation, I told you. I thought I saw you smiling, but I'm not sure because you bowed your head. I'll send you the files. There are six folders of documents. Memory came to my aid in the terrible years when absence was besieging me, and that is why it has abandoned me now. I can hardly remember any of the details anymore. They're all in those useless papers. We'll translate them, you'll be able to study them.

Then, straight afterwards, you asked me what I'm hoping for. It's the most important and most difficult of all questions, for me. But I understood what you meant to say without actually saying it, and I'm grateful to you for this, too. That there's not much to hope for, as far as Alessia and Livia are concerned. This is what I think you were thinking, and I know you're right. We can't expect much. There's a ninety percent chance that they are dead: buried in a wood, dumped at sea, I don't know. I think of them in the sea, when I can think about them at all. In the sea they could turn into fish, mermaids, baby whales. I can't tell you why: I prefer the sea to the earth. In any case, yes: it's reasonable to imagine that they were murdered. Two girls of six, old enough to speak and make demands, couldn't have spent this long without finding a way to be recognized, without asking someone where their mamma is. And they wouldn't have accepted any of the lies, even the most convincing. They're very sensitive, Alessia and Livia. Highly intelligent. They understand, they hear everything. They would have found a way, in these years of absence, to let me know: we're here. One person, a trick. Even if someone had said Mamma's dead, or Mamma doesn't want you anymore, she left. They would have come across something or someone, I think, able to capture a signal and transmit it. To be suspicious, feel sorry, understand. Paradoxically, absolute nothingness proves that they are no longer alive: nothingness and silence is evidence. I'm reading this now with your eyes, Your Honor. But you see, nothingness is not enough. Even if the probability is ninety-nine percent. Even if we're left with only a one percent chance that my twins are somewhere in the world, separated perhaps, miles away, maybe in a country where they don't speak the language, or possibly being taken care of secretly by someone who loves them, meaning their pain has been assuaged by now, perhaps they are even serene. There it is. That is the one percent that I have to pursue. It is that minuscule hypothetical probability that I'm asking you to help me explore. Whether it is valid or worthless, I still need to know. Even just to hear: there's no way. Here is the evidence, we've searched and now we have proof: the chance that they are still alive is zero. But until then, you do understand, don't you, Your Honor, all I can do is squeeze every fiber of my being into that infinitesimal space. I can't turn around and walk the other way: I am staying there.

So, the theories. We need to start from scratch, because we have nothing to work with. Can you believe it? There's not one trace, anywhere. Absolute nothingness. Mathias, the girls' father, was extremely meticulous and he didn't leave anything to chance. He sent me a letter, before killing himself, with details like where he'd left his watch in the car, where he'd parked it. But there's nothing, nothing whatsoever to confirm that the girls left with him, even though we know he bought three tickets for the Corsica ferry. No image, no witness. He smashed the GPS system in the car, he got rid of the recording device he always kept there. There were no traces of syringes, cotton wool, or drugs in the house. Nobody saw a thing. The witness statements are contradictory and unreliable. Nobody saw Alessia and Livia after one P.M. that Sunday. Nobody has ever produced a photo saying: look, here are the girls. So, where are they? Why are their soft toys there in the house, their pajamas, and not their bodies? Why were the people who could have provided some useful information—Mathias's friends, his family, our babysitter, the psychologists who had him in their care—so evasive, so fugitive? So absent. So cold in the way they handled the pain, which each of them must have felt, not as much as me, of course, but nonetheless. That's not all. It's not fair to say: it's Switzerland, Your Honor. In fact, it's embarrassing to say it, or even think it. Yes, it's true. They have a different way of showing their feelings, I know that, of course, but they know what feelings are, they run the whole gamut of emotions. Like everyone else, like each and every one of us. Let's not fall into the trap that people set for me when they used to say: she's Italian. I know the sexism, racism, and prejudice I've been subjected to. I have no intention, not even for a second, of levelling these preconceptions against somebody I can't understand—owing to my own shortcomings—just because they are not like me. I'm just saying, I'm telling you: there's something missing in the reconstruction of the facts. There's a hole that corresponds to the one I feel, magnified, inside me. A piece of the puzzle missing.

So here I am, Your Honor. I'm Italian, and so are my daughters. For me, you represent justice in my country. Justice. I'm putting my faith in you. I know it's late. I should have and could have done it sooner. I was very confused, you must understand. I was in a daze. I trusted the world around me because that was the one I had always lived in, a world without the confines of a canton. I've been naïve, unthinking, ineffectual. This is another thing I can't forgive myself for. For not having done everything I could, quickly and efficiently. I've been trying to make up for it for four years, and I'll be doing so for the rest of my life. Now that I've met you, I already feel better. Finally in the right place. My place. In my country, in my world. That's what I felt when I saw you getting out of your car with your files tucked under your arm, in the deserted car park of the courthouse on a Saturday. That you should have been at home having lunch with your family, that you must have had other plans for that day—talking to one of your children, going to the movies with your husband, studying a case, or listening to music—but that you were here, instead, with a stranger. I said to myself: here I am, I've landed where I was supposed to land. And it was true. Your manner made me proud to share the details of my story with you. The time I spent talking with you, in your chambers, made me feel as though I was where I was supposed to be. As if it were an achievement, I don't know if you know what I mean. As if I had reached the end of my leg in a relay race. As if I could pass the baton to you without losing sight of it, and trust you. Don't think I'm trying to curry your favor, I just want to speak freely and sincerely, for once. Confide in someone, entrust myself to someone. You'll run the next leg, I know you will. It doesn't matter where it will take you. The main thing is to get to the finish line, then look one another in the eye, on our knees with exhaustion, and say: well, we've done everything we can. It's all here, with us, we've done it. Later, we can say goodbye, *grazie*, and leave.

Please forgive me for making you waste even more time reading these words.

Thank you for granting me a hearing and for listening, I just wanted to say: you don't know how important this is to me. As a matter of fact, I'm sorry, of course you know.

With gratitude,

I.

17.
Dear Vittorio

Vittorio,

Do you remember that night at the Cerreto house, in our room, when you came and sat on my bed and I didn't want to talk to you? When I put my head under the blankets and I didn't want to come out? I was six, I'm sure because it was the first day of summer vacation after first grade. We'd arrived at our grandparents' place that afternoon. You were really young. I didn't want to explain anything to you, I felt this terrible pain in my body, like a massive weight on my chest that stopped me from breathing. Maybe I was sick, maybe I would die suddenly like Adelina the egg lady, I thought. I remember to this day the smell of the sheets, the warm exhalations bouncing off the linen back onto my face. The strange smell of my breath. I remember worrying that if I died in the night, you would be the one to find me and you would be frightened, and Mamma would be angry with me—though I was dead—for scaring you. It may be the earliest memory I have of the two of us when we were young. Terror. I wasn't ill, I was in love. But what did you know about love, how could I have explained it? I didn't have the words for it, anyway. I didn't even know them.

On the last day of school, Susanna showed me the ring.

This is what happened. Before leaving for the summer, Marco had given a ring to Susanna. It was made out of chicken wire, and he'd strung some beads and a real leaf, a green leaf, onto it. So you won't forget me, he'd said. At least, this is what Susanna told us girls at recess, puffed up with pride, obnoxious as ever: Marco has given me a ring for the summer, which means we're engaged the whole time until we come back to school and I'm not supposed to take it off ever, he said, even when I have a bath, so I'll remember we're a couple. She shifted her weight from one foot to the other, in her short sky-blue dress, I think, with those skinny little legs, she held her arm out in front of her and showed us the ring with the leaf. When I finally told you that night—"Leave me alone, Marco gave a ring to Susanna", "Who's Marco?", "Leave me alone", "Come on, who is it? And who's Susanna?", "Get off, you're too heavy, go back to bed"—after a while, when I thought you'd gone back to sleep and I'd started feeling scared I was going to die again, after a while you said: Iri, I'll give you a ring. Then I felt like crying. I don't know why, you'd said something really sweet. Instead, I barked back at you from under the sheets. I said: shut up, you jerk, you're my brother. Brothers and sisters don't love each other and they don't give rings. You're so dumb.

Well, Vittorio, you may not remember it at all. I've thought so many times as an adult that I should say sorry, but then I always tell myself: he doesn't remember, there's no point. Anyway, what I wanted to say is that brothers and sisters do love each other: I, for example, love you.

The other thing I wanted to tell you was that I've never in my life been in love with anyone who wasn't in love with me first. That may not have been the case with Marco's ring, it definitely wasn't. But what is certain is that I've never been in love with someone who wasn't already in love with me: as if that was a necessary precondition, I'm thinking now. A prerequisite. Never unrequited love, ever. When I listen to my friends' travails, when I read Russian novels and watch American films, I always stop and think: me, in that state, never. Do you remember Guido from senior year? That punk who was kept back a year, the school rebel? You didn't like him at all. But he chose me, out of all the other girls, and I let him choose me. Do you remember Luca at college? He was so intelligent, we used to read and study all day, we went to the film forum almost every evening, we'd started making some short films together. At one point, his mother bought an apartment for him, for us, near their house. He'd chosen me, they'd chosen me. And Hal? Do you remember Hal, the Irish guy? You used to say he looked like Anthony Perkins. It was the first year I was working abroad. Hal was really attractive, I know. He was active in politics, he wrote and traveled. All the girls loved him, I don't know why he chose me. He was a bit boring in domestic life, just so you know: very different to how he looked on the outside. We split up one Sunday morning, when we were still in bed and he was reading a biography of Stalin. I said: Hal. I think we should split up. He said: I think it's a good idea, and went on reading. He always did what I wanted in the end. He was pretty docile.

I let myself be chosen by the others, too. By all of them, including David, who wanted me to go live with him in Indiana and convert to Judaism: do you remember how wonderful his parents were? His mother Vera, was a con-centration camp survivor. Vera, what a woman. Nonna

Klara adored her. I gave Alessia her name, her second name. David, too, chose me, wanted me, claimed me.

But, do you know what, Vittorio? None of them ever gave me a ring. I was thinking about it yesterday: why not? Maybe the idea was floated from time to time and I wasn't interested, I have no idea. I have no memory of rings. And yet, there's no better gift, right? To give to someone you love. As Marco said to Susanna: here's a ring, to remember we're a couple. That's always with you, on your body, that encircles, holds, consoles, and encourages you, that's both a secret and a showcase. A commitment, a promise. It's the only thing to give when you're in love, don't you think? There's nothing like it. Nothing else. See what a discovery I've made, at almost fifty! Don't tell anyone, will you? Please. Not even Orsola. Promise me.

Well, Vic. The truth is that I'm writing to you to tell you this: Luis gave me a ring yesterday. I wanted to call you straight away, but there was the time difference and I couldn't. I don't think I've ever been so happy. I wanted to say these words out loud to you, without any shame. I've never been happier. Does that sound sacrilegious to you? I know, I know. But let me live the moment without spoiling it. A moment of incredible joy, perfect joy. Luis said: try it on, it's nothing special, but it seemed right for you, I saw it and I thought: it's so like her, it looks like her. Nothing special, he said. Do you know what it is? A ring of leaves. Leaves, can you believe it? With a lurch, I felt disoriented: I fell through an air pocket of more than forty years, back to that night, I saw you in bed, I could smell the sheets and hear you speaking. I should have called you straight away. But Luis was there, his eyes imploring: What's wrong? Don't you like it? So, I let him put it on my finger, I felt as though I was six years old, and I thought that I've never loved a man as much as I love him. Ever.

Except you, of course. But brothers and sisters don't give one another rings, beloved little brother. Do you remember? Jerk . . .

I'm hugging you so tight it'll suffocate you, torturing you with tickles, and kissing you all over your face even though you hate it, I'll force you to let me kiss you, because I'm older than you, I'm stronger, and you can't do anything about it. Say please, or I'll never leave you alone.

I'm expecting you, baby bro. Come and see my ring. Come soon.

Love.

18.
NORMA

There are infinite opportunities for presenting yourself as irreproachable in Switzerland. Norma has never missed a trick in that department. My first impression was that she was like a perfect machine. She was quite a striking phenomenon. I observed her as an anthropologist would upon coming across a completely unknown tribe that had never been recorded before. I almost took notes. Her hours, her habits, her clothes, her words. The sequence of her gestures. There was never a wrong move. The final result was wrong, but each of her gestures was gauged to perfection. I would actually have liked to learn from her. Yes, for self-defense, if I ever needed it. I didn't manage, though. There was a secret I was unable to decipher. At the same time, I didn't let her get to me, either. I didn't get upset, I was never offended. At the end of the day, she made me laugh. Or rather: she would have really made me laugh if she hadn't been Mathias's mother. When she was around, he was like an animal pricking up its ears for sounds humans can't detect. Vigilant, watchful, alarmed, present and absent at the same time. Tuning in someplace else. Missing, but completely collected.

I can't remember a single reproach or criticism. And yet, her disapproval was absolute. How did my mother-in-law always manage to be so harsh without ever stopping smiling? And anyway, why was she so harsh? With the girls, she would rattle off a string of orders disguised as kindness. She anticipated their wishes in order to thwart them. She would suggest one thing on purpose to obtain the opposite. It was lethal. It worked.

I wouldn't really be able to give you any examples. None of them do her justice. They were little things. If she saw me holding one of the girls while the other was on the floor, she'd always peel the one I was holding out of my arms. She'd never pick up the one on the carpet. She'd walk over and take the little girl away from me. She'd plonk her on the floor and only then would she pick up the other one.

When she had too much food in the fridge, for example too many eggs—she often complained that the farmer gave her too many eggs—she'd say to me: come on, take some home and make a cake for Alessia and Livia. She'd keep the fresh eggs and give me the supermarket ones with the date stamped on them. Near their expiry date, never actually expired.

When she brought over clothes for the girls, she'd wrap them in beautiful boxes and say: these are from my friends. They were worn-out, frayed, secondhand T-shirts. I don't know where she found them. I'm pretty sure her friends didn't give them to her. But the boxes were magnificent.

Once, at the table during lunch, she treated us to an interminable spiel about how the real problem in Swiss schools, the decay of teaching standards, was that kids spoke Italian in the playground. *Die Kinder sprechen Italienisch*. She said it, to me, in German.

Nothing, really. Little things.

19

DEAR TEACHER

Dear Teacher,
I called the school office asking if I could have Alessia and Livia's schoolwork—their compositions, tests, exercise books, and drawings—but they explained that the material was the property of the school and that copies can only be obtained in genuine cases of demonstrable necessity and only by following a specific procedure. When I asked what "genuine cases of demonstrable necessity" might be, they were unable to give me any concrete examples. I suppose transferring to a school in another country that requires the material as a condition for registering, the secretary finally suggested, worn down by my insistence. I thought for a moment about doing it. Enrolling Alessia and Livia in a French school, or an Italian one. The hoops I would have to jump through flashed for an instant in my mind. I couldn't face it. Ultimately, behaving as if the girls and I, the three of us, actually had a new school year ahead of us would have been a deadly trap. In certain moments I might have ended up believing it. Because, you see, dear Teacher: Alessia and Livia will not be going back to school in September. They will not be enrolling in second grade. So, this is the reality we have to reckon with: we need to stay within it, without forgetting but without going crazy with

the memory, without living eternally in the past, trying to imagine a future. Do these count as "genuine cases of demonstrable necessity"? I don't think there's a case history to refer to. I understand that in the absence of precedents, it's not easy to be the first person to make a decision. I'm aware that this is creating a problem for the school board, and I apologize. However, my "demonstrable necessity" at the moment is to stay alive. I have at least one good reason: as long as I'm alive, Alessia and Livia are alive with me. In order to achieve this—to stay alive day after day—I need to preserve their things as they were. As they left them, all their things. Their clothes and toys, their shoes—I can't explain why, but their shoes are the most impossible things to part from. Nobody can walk barefoot here in Switzerland, can they? Shoes are essential. In addition, I need their drawings and the words they wrote down, their thoughts. I need to go over them, sort them out. Read them to myself, every now and again. See them once more. That's it, you see. I hope I'll be able to fill in the form, making a mighty effort to summarize in one line what my "genuine case of demonstrable necessity" is. In the meantime, I'd like to illustrate it for you.

In fact, it's you I have to ask, they told me when I finally managed to find out what the "specific procedure" was. The first step is a *nihil obstat* from the class teacher. Your authorization, dear Teacher. It is required that you confirm there are no obstacles. That you do not create any, either, I suppose.

This is why, after such a long silence, I have resolved to write to you. Whether I will be able to get hold of Alessia and Livia's schoolwork again is up to you: I'm thinking especially of a composition with the title "Who I am," which we read together when they brought it home to show me their marks, and which made me cry with happiness. Their drawings, too. There must be the pictures where they drew themselves with braids—one in a circle, the other in a triangle, an extraordinary way to depict themselves as completely different—as well as the one with the blue house, and that other one where the family is on a picnic at the lake. Then, of course, the math problems. The sums, I remember in particular, with the Tens and Units written in different colors. We'd bought the pencils the day before because Livia said you, dear Teacher, wanted the ones with thicker tips: ours, the ones in their pencil cases, were too fine. These are the things I feel I need to preserve and cherish.

I don't deny that telling you all this makes me uncomfortable, and I want to be honest with you: I haven't been able to understand your silence in these months. I've also suffered because of it, though it wasn't at the top of my list of sources of pain. But whenever my thoughts have turned to school, and therefore to the girls at school, and to their teacher—to you, that is—it has occurred to me to wonder what the reasons for your absence might be. You must have had a lot of difficulties with the class, I can imagine them, you've had to see the horror in the eyes of the twins' classmates and explain to them what happened: you must have had to try and find the right words. Then you may perhaps have thought it wasn't the right moment. Then, discretion may have taken over. Respect.

I've been remembering my own teacher: she was Italian and she was very discreet, too. My "dear Teacher," Francesca. I remember her perfume, that smelled of oriental spices. Tall, elegant. I wanted to be like her. She spoke softly, sweetly. So many years have gone by, but I remember her as clearly as if I could see her, exactly as if I could hear her right now. Alessia and Livia must have loved you, too: they must have listened in awe to your explanations, your readings, your advice on how to learn a poem off by heart. Children's memories, they're so amazing. I'm thinking about all that time when I was not with the girls but you were, all those moments of their lives that you preserve: made up of surprises, unfamiliar names and concepts, worlds unfolding, revealing themselves for the first time. I envy you a little. What a wonderful calling, what a supreme undertaking yours is.

Well, dear Teacher. Whatever your reasons for not being able, or willing, to get in touch with me over these months, please be assured that we don't need to talk about it, to ask or give any explanations. I only hope that your silence isn't your way of expressing your disapproval: this is the only thing I wouldn't be able to understand. Many people have stayed away, lots have secretly censured, judged, and issued their verdicts condemning me. It's easy to look at other people's lives, take fifteen minutes to declare them guilty, go home, safe in the certainty you are right, and go straight to sleep. Anyone can do it, some people have to: a judge, an arbiter, a witness. A teacher, I believe, is made of different stuff. My teacher was different. She always used to say: you're all right but now maybe it's better if we try and do things this other way. People always have their reasons. Now, maybe it's better if we try and find a way. I don't know what "this other way" is, today. I'm just asking you, dear Teacher, to keep your door open. Following the procedure, maybe, we'll find an opening that will lead us to an answer.

Please know that for all the time that you've devoted to my daughters, I am always, and will forever be, very grateful.

I.

20.
LIST. MEMORY

Things I mustn't forget

1. In bed at night when I was little in the Castagneto house, with Vittorio in the bed beside me. My place in the world, what I thought it was. The chill of damp sheets, the heat of embers: together.
2. That time doesn't exist. We're all part of the world at the same time, in the past, present, and future.
3. That there's no point in explaining this. Some people know it, others don't but there's no point.
4. The rules of good health: sleep at least six hours, respect your body, take care of it. Spend at least ten minutes a day listening to it and understanding what it wants. Do some exercise, walk. Don't take any medication unless absolutely necessary. Unless. Absolutely. Necessary.
5. Call Nonna. Write a few lines to her every day and send her one letter a week.
6. The power of music. Llasa de Sela's voice.
7. The power of reading. A book, wherever I am, with me, always.
8. The power of fairy tales. Don't abandon the project of translating that collection of fairy tales from all over the world. Don't give up. Insist even when it feels really tiring, painful.

9. Todo cuadra. This formula, everything adds up. But you can't really translate it. Everything is as it should be. You don't need to keep on moving the pieces around. You only need to watch them moving, see where they go. This is what we are: active spectators in the theater of the universe. Life is a show, it really is. Todo cuadra.

10. Love is fragile. It's something that is so magic that you need to be really careful. About how you say things. Otherwise, it fades, it dies. It has to stay beautiful. It lives off smiles. Handle with care. Control your obsessions, don't make scenes with pointless jealousy. Most importantly, don't test it. Ever.

11. Trick words. Tantrum. Fault. Rule. Danger. Don't play with these words. When it feels like others know the rules of the game and you don't. When they want to make you think you're inadequate, and you end up believing them. When they want to make you say you're a spoilt little girl, that you played with fire. That's it's your fault. Your. Fault. That you weren't careful, you didn't see the danger. Selfish. Blind. You should have dealt with it. Don't play with these words. Don't touch them. They're deadly traps.

12. When I came out of Barnes & Noble, where I'd been looking for a guide to New York. September 11, 2001. The looks of the people around me as they turned to look at the smoke billowing down the street and said, maybe it's a fire. You never understand history while it's unfolding. It's rare. Vera, David's mother, said the same thing about when they were deported to the camp: you don't understand right away, it's rare. Big history is a little shift in your life. It's the little history of your life that is big.

21.
PAPA

He was born in Castagneto, in the province of Ascoli. The eldest of four. His father, Giuseppe, was the chief magistrate in the region. His mother, my grandmother, Mayme, died two weeks before I was born. I carry her first name as my second. My grandmother was the daughter of an American woman, born in Kenosha, Wisconsin, the city where Orson Welles was born. She was taken to Italy by her father in exchange for a great deal of money. With that money, with the money he took to leave the country with his little daughter and abandon the woman he loved, my great grandfather bought his land in Italy. There was a kind of original sin—the terrible distress of a mother whose baby girl was torn from her arms—behind his fortune.

Over the next generations we've all given something back, which has ended up in that deep well. Papa had three motorbikes, they were his passion. When he was twenty-four, he lost a leg in an accident. Pietro, his name is Pietro. Nothing stops him. The strength I have is passed down from him. He studied engineering and became an agronomist. In the 1960s, he went to work in Brussels. That's where he met my mother, Astrid, who was the secretary of a colleague. An Italian, missing a leg. My German grandfather—of course—was against the marriage. They went through with it anyway. I was born not long after, Irina Mayme. They called me Irina because it sounded Italian in Germany, but Northern European in Italy. Then my brother Vittorio was born. My father was very different with him. He let him do what he wanted. With me, he was overbearing and quick-tempered. He kept me in his sights, and put a lid on me, as if I were a cooking pot. If he didn't like what I was wearing, he'd tell me to go and change. When I spoke, I always had the impression that he was ignoring what I was saying. When there was an argument, he'd say: you just need to shut up. He said I provoked him. He was prey to fits of anger and there was no way to negotiate with him. My mother couldn't leave him, she tolerated him. Whenever she could, she'd flee to my grandmother's. I remember once. I must have been around fourteen. My radio was broken, my brother had two sets. I asked him for one, and he said no. I took it anyway. He went and complained to my father. Papa came into my room: give that radio back to your brother. I said no and he gave me a slap. Give it back. No. Another slap. Again, and again, I don't know how many times, but a lot. Like when a film is jammed in the reel. In the end, I gave it back.

I don't know why, but he always seemed angry.

I wanted to study Art History. He said: do you want to stand on your own two feet? Let's make a pact. I'll pay for college, you study Law. He was right. He was the one that decided to enroll me in the Italian section of the International School in Brussels. He wanted me to be first and foremost Italian. As soon as I turned eighteen, my mother took me aside and said: you have to leave. And I did.

He was extremely harsh with me, but he was a good

man. I'm sure of one thing: he loved me a lot. After
Mathias took the girls away and then killed himself, Papa
came to my room one day, grabbed hold of my shoulders
and shook me. He said: you mustn't die, don't allow yourself to do something like that to yourself or to me. You
mustn't die, he wanted to kill you but you won't do it, you
will not die. It was then, at that very moment—looking at
myself through my father's eyes—that I realized that no, I
wouldn't die. I couldn't do that to him, he was right, I
couldn't do that to myself. To my daughters. He's always
been right.

I sometimes think that the fact that I was habituated to
violence as an ordinary thing between people—as a way of
expressing bonds of love—made it harder for me to rec-
ognize abuse as an adult. Saying this about my father,
though, costs me an enormous effort, I don't know whether
I can do it. It costs me even more than talking about my
girls. I think this is truly the hardest thing. I don't think I'll
ever be able to tell him. Because my father loves me
immensely, I'm sure of it. He's a wonderful person, I owe
so much of what I am to him. No, I can't reproach him for
anything. He was harsh, but he had a point. He was right.
He loved me. He loves me.

22.
A DREAM

I'm always dreaming about water, fish, whales. Mostly whales.

Once, though, I had a dream that was so vivid it felt true and I wrote it down in the morning. It must have really happened, somewhere.

I was up in the hills, just after sunset. The hill was bare, there were no trees, only bushes, lots of bushes. The sky was orange. I had to get away from something, I don't know what, and I had two newborn babies in my arms. They were really heavy, I couldn't run with both of them in my arms. So, I thought: I'll hide one of them behind a bush and carry the other to safety, then come back. But when I came back, I couldn't find the one I'd left behind. I looked desperately until I found it. Then I picked it up and went back to where I'd left the other. But I couldn't find the first one where I'd left it, behind another bush at the bottom of the hill. So, with the second one in my arms, I started looking for the first, but the baby was heavy and I had to put it down. I finally found the first one, huge relief, happiness, but right away panic about having left the second one. I couldn't find it. I kept losing one of them. I don't know how many times. On and on, without end.

I was thinking, as I was writing the dream down to make peace with it, that when I found out I was pregnant with twins I found it hard to imagine them together, or speaking to them together. When you speak, you usually speak to one person at a time. Except for political rallies, of course, but there you're in front of a throng of strangers. When you speak to someone you love, I mean, it's always one on one. It's hard to imagine saying I love you to two people together. I found it really hard, when I was pregnant, to say to the two of them at the same time: I love you. Speaking to both, sometimes, is too much. You don't feel competent. You don't feel up to it. You don't know who to ask for help.

23.
ME ABOUT YOU. BORDER

You've been looking for them for years. I need to be sure I've done everything possible, you say. I can't leave the door open to any doubt. You founded an association in Switzerland. A foundation whose mission, in their name, is to find missing children. You've never stopped. You fear they're dead, ultimately you think they are, at times you say they are. You don't have their bodies, though. Grief in the absence of a body is a mysterious and unrelenting hemorrhage: there's always new lifeblood ready to seep out, ready to regenerate, it never depletes itself. I've seen mothers in Argentina look for their children for thirty years. I've also seen grandmothers find their missing grand-children after forty years, and it's a sight that cannot be described. Especially their eyes. The skin on their face relaxing as if it were new, and their eyes shining.

I need to pass the border from shadow into light, you say distractedly while you're washing a glass.

24.
Me About You. Details

You want to talk about you. About what you're like now. You want to say, eyes wide with surprise, that it can happen, something you would never have imagined possible has happened to you. Love is back, it never really left: it was hidden in a corner, crouching in fear with its hands over its head, but it was there. You're berated for it. You should be in mourning for eternity, people say without saying: how shameful to forget your own daughters. But you tilt your head and smile with your young girl's teeth: they don't know what they're talking about. It's impossible to forget, but you have to live because that's what nature has decided: pain on its own doesn't kill you. The absence of love can be repaired by new love. You talk and talk. You talk about changes. Memories. You wonder. How was it possible for someone like you—a hugely successful attorney, an executive at a multinational company, a cultured and cosmopolitan woman with a great deal of life experience—how was it possible, I repeat, not to see that the man you lived with was coercive and controlling. We get stuck on this point a lot, we keep asking one another questions. Was there abuse? No, not physically at least. There was harshness, at times. In his character. A certain coldness. He was precise, preemptive, rigorous, prudent. Reliable, for all these reasons:

a great organizer, a man who would think of everything, a guarantee. Incredibly attentive to the girls, his daughters: a constant presence. Were there signals? No, there weren't. Or maybe there were, of course there were, but I didn't see them for what they were. An obsessive-compulsive personality, the experts later decreed. Do you know what this means? How does a man like this behave? He pairs his socks before putting them in the washing machine, he loads the dishwasher with the plates in decreasing size, he's compulsive about order but only his own, he places his things on his desk the same way every time, he plans his days in a notebook, he turns garbage recycling into a ritual. Laugh, Irina. The world's full of men like that. Men who can't accept uncertainty, who attempt to control events as if they were life's traffic police. He was an engineer, Mathias. A German Swiss engineer, go on, laugh. A yachtsman, loved by his friends, brilliant. A manipulator, for sure. A man who manages to bring everyone over to his side. He managed with me, too. A chess player who gives you a glass of wine and tells you a funny story while he's driving you into a corner, but you don't feel like you're in a corner, you feel like you are exactly where you wanted to be. Do you see what I mean? You talk and talk. You say there were a few more sinister details, but that's all they were, details, and it's not like every man with a profile like his goes missing with their kids. And anyway, you need to be careful, yes, that's it, you need to be careful not to normalize the fact that there's some new little persecution every day, some rule that is so petty and incomprehensible that you basically accept it, you need to be careful not to withdraw without realizing you're doing so, until you end up in a place that is no longer yours but it is too late, by

then. Because that is what happened to me, you say. I real-
ized I was no longer me, but there were the girls to think
about and it was too late.

I used to think: be patient, it'll pass.

25.
To Monsieur M.

To Monsieur M.
Senior Prosecutor and Head of Investigations in the district of L.

Dear Monsieur M.,
First of all, I would like to I apologize for writing to you, but since we first met many months ago it has been impossible to obtain an appointment to see you in person. If I'd known our first meeting was to be our last, I would have done things better. I mean, I would have attempted—even though I was "overly emotional," as you pointed out—to be more precise, clear, and pertinent in my requests. That is what I will try to be now, in writing.

I was indeed overly emotional back then, and I cannot deny that I still am. I realize that the investigative unit of the police force in your district must have a huge case-load, criminal activities compared to which the disappearance of two six-year-old girls in the distant past deserves to go into the cold-case file. In fact, this is precisely what spurred me to write to you now: a brief memo from your office informing me that, owing to the negative outcome of your investigation, the case is being archived. My counter-signature is required, I am told, in order to close the case officially. Closing the case is necessary for "further formalities" to be undertaken, the telegraphic missive concludes. The most important of these formalities, I cannot imagine otherwise, is a declaration of presumed death, without which the assets deriving from the estate of the girls' father's family, in the absence of descendants, cannot be distributed.

You must understand my difficulty in signing, respected Monsieur M. It's not the inheritance, of course: there's no need for me to clarify the fact that I would not have been the beneficiary in any case. You know—it's in all the deeds—and it pains me even to put pen to paper on the subject. It's the presumed death. I beg you to consider, even though the role you play obliges you to keep a necessary and mandatory distance from the state of mind of the people with whom you come into contact, that it is absolutely impossible for me to counter-sign a declaration of the kind without first knowing for sure that no stone has been left unturned in ascertaining the facts and the truth. I do not know, we do not know, what actually happened. In my view, the investigation has left a few important questions open, which, with the greatest respect, I would like to bring to your attention. I will summarize these in the following bullet points.

- Homicidal intentions. In our only meeting, you appeared to have interpreted my last email to Mathias, the girls' father, as being a trigger for his "desperation"—that is what you called it—implying that a man in a state of prostration of this kind could have been driven to extremes. Do you realize what you wrote, you asked me. I'm attaching the email, dated January 26, 2011, because I want to save you the bother of looking it up in the file. Please read it again. You will find that it simply shares information and that there is a hint of affection there, of collaboration, even. For that matter, our separation was not dramatic, there had never been any conflict between us. I'd like to remind you that just before they went missing, the girls had been on vacation with their father in the Caribbean for three whole weeks. Three weeks was a much longer period than the custody agreement had stipulated. We decided together, my ex-husband and I, that Livia and Alessia would enjoy the trip; we established together that it was the right decision. On their return, we went back to our everyday routine, without any grievances. Until the Sunday they went missing, nothing could have made me think that Mathias harbored any other intentions than those of a good father.

- The therapists. This point—his homicidal intentions, Mathias's real state of mind—could have been taken to the experts for potential confirmation. The therapist in whose care he had been for some time, for example, who saw him on Thursday, just three days before the disappearance. She has never been called as a witness, with the excuse that she lives and works in another district: red tape, procedural problems. A formal rogatory letter between the two cantons would have been required, I discovered. It was considered unnecessary. Similarly, someone from the station phoned the couples' therapist whom we saw for some time together, just before the separation. She said that she couldn't give any information if not in person, and implored them to come and interview her. Nobody went. If they had had something important to tell us, they would have called, one of your colleagues told me. Thus, we have no proof whatsoever regarding Mathias's real psychological and physical state.

- The boots. Having established that nothing induces us to believe that my ex-husband had homicidal intentions, I think we need to come up with some evidence. Our neighbors said they saw him wearing his muddy trekking boots when he went to pick up the girls at lunchtime. Might he have gone that morning to a place in the countryside or in the woods? Where? Why? I found the boots at home, I brought them to the station so that the soil on the treads could be analyzed. They told me that earth is the same everywhere. The samples were never analyzed.

- The house. It has never been formally searched. I can't help wondering whether there are objects, fingerprints, traces that might help us determine what Mathias was planning. For weeks, dozens of people traipsed in and out whenever they liked. I wonder whether there might have been, might still be, something that would help the investigation.

- The phone card. I had to guarantee an advance fee of 900 Swiss Francs before they would put a trace on Mathias's phone and find his position on the Sunday of the disappearance. I never received the list of his incoming and outgoing calls. Who did he speak to? How many times? For how long? I think this is relevant.

- The family. In the five days between his disappearance and his death, as you know, nobody in Mathias's family came to Saint-Simon to take part in the search or help in any way. We know nothing about their activities during those days, or afterwards. It would be important to find out, I believe.

- The kidnapping alert. The Swiss police never alerted their French or Italian counterparts that a kidnapping had taken place. The car was driven tens of thousands of kilometers without anyone doing anything to stop its journey. The car was in my name: a simple car-theft report would have been enough to warrant a search.
- The sightings. A witness that was considered reliable said they saw the girls with their father at Lyon airport on the Sunday they disappeared. I ask myself, and I ask you, whether the flight manifests for that airport were ever inspected, and I have no evidence that they were, to check that there weren't any unaccompanied minors on any flights, and if there were, authorized by whom, towards which destination?
- The sailing bags. As I reported to your agents, two big sailing bags that used to be in the wardrobe at home had vanished. Mathias was a skilled sailor, he had a yacht moored at the lake. He kept his gear in those bags. I found his stuff, in the wardrobe, but not the bags. Do you have any idea what shape and size sailing bags are? A giant canvas sack, more than a meter long, with a cord drawstring. Actually. Two. He emptied them both and disappeared with them.

There are many other questions that I have been racking my brains about in these months, respected Monsieur M., but I don't want to trouble you with suppositions. It's just that the rebuttal I receive from your unit every time I make a request—"your husband was German Swiss, not Brazilian," "your husband was the girls' father, he would have cared about what happened to them"—continues to feel like insufficient reason to close the case. At least from my point of view, which I hope you are willing to consider relevant. I will therefore not counter-sign the application. I am, on the contrary, asking you here today to permit the investigation to be taken further, possibly in collaboration with your counterparts in the relevant countries. However late in the day, new enquiries could yield results. Whatever they are: they may even bring us the closure we've never had.

I trust in your collaboration, your understanding, and offer my cordial greetings.

Wishing you the best success,

I.L.

26.
TIME

A t the end of that same year, I left. Ten months later. Ten months on medication: sleeping tablets, tranquillizers, antidepressants, sedatives. A time with no day or night, cotton-wool time.

Go. Go alone. Go far away, towards water. Don't take anything, a bag with some books, a notebook, a pair of shoes. Don't require anything. Ask for hospitality, in villages, like a traveler. Walk and walk. Asia. A dot on the map, the memory of a remote trip years ago. Yogyakarta, Java. An island not too far away. Sulawesi. Four spans of earth in the sea.

I'd never held my head underwater before. Not like that, I mean: diving, deep diving. But in that village, there was a signpost and the sign advertised a guide. Have you ever been underwater? I thought it would be dark, but it never is. The fish swim in schools, organized by color, by race. The seabed is like mountain scenery, a secret topography. All I can say is there's a sense of peace. As if nature were somehow better there. There's silence. You're suspended: as if you were flying, held up by the water. You rise and fall with your breath. The air expands and you rise. You feel a little giddy, at times. In the silence, every now and again, a kind of music, a faint, stifled melody.

When you move, everything glimmers. Immense, perfect harmony. Boundless liberty. You are vulnerable, defense-less. You are nothing, and yet you finally feel like yourself. Your whole, weightless-yet-solid self. Human endeavor suddenly feels like part of another universe. Coherent, mysterious.

Life is very simple. To be happy, you need very little. To be happy, you need hardly anything. Nothing, in any case, that is not already inside you.

Water cured me. I dove in one day and came out much later, I have no idea when. I had lost my memory of the small things, the details had vanished. When, at what time, what day, who. All gone. No before, no after. All that remained was a sharp and luminous memory of what I loved and still love, all in the here and now. Time is our prison. The too soon, the too late, the too short, the too lit-tle.

In that time without time, I met Luis.

27.
LUIS

L uis has long fingers, so long it's hard to believe they're his. The first time I saw him take his hands out of his pockets, I thought he must have inherited them from some ancestor. A Greek great-great-grandfather perhaps. Armenian. Or Andalusian. But what do I know about Andalusian hands? Greek, I decided.

You can't tell how old Luis is. At times, when the veins pulsate in his temples, he looks incredibly old, and you'd like him to sit you on his lap and tell you all about life. Other times, when he laughs with all his white teeth, you'd like to sit him in your lap and say: come here, little boy, don't be scared. I'll hold you, come here.

Luis isn't scared of pain. Neither his nor other people's. He knows it well: he accepts it lovingly, as if it were a friend. He handles it with confidence and with respect. He addresses it with the intimate *Tu*, but always with a capital T.

He is never embarrassed about his bodily fluids. This is surprising in a man. Blood tears sweat urine feces. When he's dirty, he cleans himself, when he cuts himself, he heals. He cries often, sweats profusely. Everything he came across the moment he came into the world is naturally part of his world, forever.

Luis, in fact, is not a man. Not just a man, I mean. There's a woman hiding inside him.

He never says no. At most, he says: it's possible. That's his way of indicating a difficulty. That it's not easy. It's not certain. It wasn't planned. It's really complicated. Therefore, it's possible.

The first thing he gave me was a set of keys to his house. We hardly knew one another. The keyring was in the shape of a whale. Once, many months before, in a brief aside in an email, I'd mentioned that I often dreamed about whales. It was just an aside. A few words.

His memory is prodigious. He remembers everything. A tune he's only heard once, a conversation at a nearby table, pages of a book, anecdotes from the distant past. Names of people he's bumped into by chance. Looks, intentions, sequences, the color of clothes, unexpressed thoughts, unfinished ones. It's as if his memory were boundless. As if it already contains everything, and all he has to do is retrieve an item. He plunges in, picks it up, and reemerges. He's a reef diver.

He entertains me, takes me out of myself, makes me laugh a lot. He makes me cry, too. When the crying comes, he lets me cry: he's there, calm and silent. When it's over, he takes my hand and says: let's go now.

When I said, that day: don't you have a bidet in your

bathroom? I wanted to take it back immediately. What a stupid thing to say: I could see there wasn't one. I said sorry, and smiled. A week later, he'd installed one. He said: of course, I did it myself. I don't believe him, but it could be true. He could actually have done it himself. It doesn't matter, I know, but I often think about it. He may have picked up a pickaxe, soldered the pipes. Who knows?

Luis runs, cycles, treks in the woods, swims for hours. He has the stamina of a wild animal. For good measure, he smokes and drink red wine.

The one time I saw him get angry, absolutely furious, with his son, he didn't say: you're an idiot. He said: *estas muy equivocado*. You're making a big mistake. Not "you're wrong" but "there's something wrong with what you're doing." It's different.

He's exceptionally talented in his work, but he doesn't know it. Not completely. He knows he can do things well, that he has a gift. He brings his drawings to life, he can see that. But if you tell him, you capture the soul of things, you give life beyond life, he'll shrug and say stop it, leave off.

Sometimes he vanishes, and then he comes back. He never puts you to the test, you're never under examination. As a consequence: you never put him to the test. There's no point, he is what he is, and he's always there. Even when he's not.

I've been in love many times in my life. I've known desire passion need for tenderness compassion sharing comradeship harmony jealousy heartbreak desperation and the peaceful joy of daily life. I thought I'd loved a great deal and I'd never love again. I was wrong.

I think I've only just now understood what love is.

28.
LIVIA. ALESSIA

No. I don't have a single picture with me. I don't have one in my wallet. I don't need to see them captured and immobilized in the past. I see them alive in the present, I don't even need to close my eyes. I see them and hear them. No photo looks like a person who is alive. In the photo they are still. In real life, even when you are still, you are breathing. Photos don't breathe.

No. More than difficult, it's impossible, it feels like there's no point trying to describe them. I would use adjectives loaded with significance for me, but empty for everyone else. What does "Livia is more introverted, Alessia is softer," mean to you? Categories, boxes. For me, on the other hand, every word is a sequence of gestures, body movements, tiny episodes, looks. Livia is stronger, more independent. Alessia is more sensitive and insecure. You see? It doesn't mean a thing. If anything, I'd like to be able to explain the physical sensation I felt every day when I held them in my arms. That combination of impetus and surrender children's bodies have when they allow you to pick them up. Livia was always in one piece, whole. With an internal vertical uprightness, I don't know how to describe it. She was always herself. But Alessia would spread herself out, she would mold herself to my body. She would become me. They had different consistencies. You could tell from the way they let themselves be hugged what kind of people they would turn into.

No. There isn't one image in particular that comes to mind. Every single one. All my memories are here: it's not that they return, they never left. They haven't been dislodged since the second they came into the world. They move around, for sure. Sometimes you're surprised by the moment when they manifest themselves to you. I mean, you're not expecting them. The other evening, while I was locking the front door, I was assailed by a memory from that afternoon at the lake. The girls must have been about three, we were cycling and Alessia couldn't get her bike going. I had been kneeling by her front wheel for a while. I fiddled with the brakes, the leads. I was looking for the problem. Little Livia came up to me, her full height as tall as me crouching. She said: Mamma, Alessia's bike isn't working because the handlebars are the wrong way round. There it was, in a breath. While I was locking the front door the other evening.

29.
To Philippe

To Philippe R
32, Rue de Savoie
Paris VI

D earest Philippe,
There's no such thing as coincidences, you always used to say with a laugh when we went out in the evening and I told you, at our bistro table, how amazed I was at the numbers, names, and places that have recurred over the course of my life. There's no such thing, Irina: the tangles of life are sticking in your comb, as you Italians would say, that's all. For some, the tangles get stuck, for others, the comb simply slips through. Some people don't even bother combing their hair, you said laughing even harder and pouring me another drink.

It was the first image that flashed through my mind when I heard about the attack on the offices of your newspaper. Before calling you, before finding it in my heart to tap in your number and wait for an answer—or perhaps no answer, please let there be an answer—I saw the teeth in your smile, the half-light of those evenings, the iron chairs on the sidewalk, your hands. There's no such thing as coincidences. Come on, let's go home.

So, you are fine it seems, or as well as you can be

considering what happened. I remember those rooms filled with papers, drawings, cardboard tubes resting in the corners. We went, you took me, just before I left Paris. You were the last person I saw, the last eyes mine locked with—at the airport—before leaving to start a new life. A position that was so prestigious I couldn't say no, in Lausanne. Do you remember? You can't refuse, Irina. You must go. Don't think about us now, go and then see. We'll meet again.

There you have it. You at the newspaper office, you now. All these years. Well, there may be no such thing as coincidences, but there's also no such thing as time, right? It's an invention, a unit of measurement that has been selected from millions of possible ones. You would always laugh when I said: I'll never forget the dates of my transfers, I won't be able to. I came to Paris the first time—what day was it?—the day before Lady Di was killed in the Alma tunnel, on August 30, 1997. I arrived in New York—what day, what month?—the day before the attack on the Twin Towers. It was September 10, 2001. The following day I came out of a Barnes & Noble, where I'd gone to buy a guidebook, and everyone outside the store was looking up and yelling: there's a fire. Alessia and Livia's date of birth—but you know this already—is October 7, the same as Nonna Mayme's, whose name is mine and whose mother's destiny I share. When they were born, you sent me a greeting card with the message: *everything comes around*. Well, it does. Come around.

I've never really told you about Propriano. A place I'd never even heard of before finding out, during the investigation, that Mathias landed in this little town on Corsica on the first leg of his journey: he had taken a ferry from

Marseilles to Propriano. Alessia and Livia may have been with him, but all we know is that he bought three tickets. We also know for certain that he later traveled from Propriano to Toulon alone. That means—the investigators said—that if the girls did actually get on the ferry and if— assuming they did get on the ferry—they also got off, then Propriano would be the place where someone could have picked them up and taken them away. In short, this place I'd never heard of had suddenly become vitally important. The center of the world.

A long, long time afterwards, I left for Indonesia. I met two people there, a man and a woman. The man was Luis, you know all about him. The woman was a friend of his, a Spaniard like him, I thought. And yet, when we sat down at a table over there on the other side of the world, under a volcano, she started telling me about herself and the first thing she said was this: I actually come from Corsica. I was born in Propriano. There and then, I thought I'd misunderstood. I said: where? She repeated it. Out of all the places in the world: Propriano.

Okay, Philippe. There's no such thing as coincidences. You're right, comme d'habitude. There are desires and passions that carry us along and bind us, designated or invisible routes we follow, tangles, combs, hair. Well, my hair is short now, I hardly need a comb. My hands are enough to keep it in shape. Hands for writing to each other, for hugging each other. To wave when we're in the arrivals hall at the airport. I'll come and see you soon, or you come and see me. I miss you.

I.

30.
Me About You. Switzerland

Then you want to talk about Switzerland. Warn the whole world about Switzerland, tell people how to survive Switzerland, and this is the afternoon that makes us laugh the most, of all the ones we've spent together. You should write a self-help manual, you say—gleefully getting up to get a drink, rinsing out the glasses from before—it would be the most sensible thing to do, for sure: a handbook for those who are obliged to live in Switzerland for work, or as a result of other random life choices, so that they will know, especially people from the South, what they will encounter and how to defend themselves if they are employed by a Swiss company, or if they fall in love with a Karl, a Mathias, or a Rose. People have no idea, you say.

You, who have traveled everywhere in the world, lost your way in Switzerland. You, who have I don't know how many degrees, who speak I don't know how many languages, who have dealt with I don't know how many sharks in the world of international finance, were forced to surrender to those two policemen—you pour a glass of wine, and laugh with your head cocked to one side, you almost apologize because you still can't believe it. Even when you talk about the disastrous investigation, which was incoherent, chaotic, disorderly, and delayed, even when you say they, the *police, treated you with contempt because you were Italian and, worse, female, whereas your husband was both Swiss and male, you can't help imitating the pair of bumbling cops you had to deal with, and they're so easy to imagine, one tall one short, one skinny one fat, sitting there at their pristine, uncluttered desks. You reenact their voices, their accents, their looks. And when you talk about the caricature of power, about the chief prosecutor in the canton who, when an authorization is needed in another canton, ten kilometers away, requires a formal international rogatory: impossible, madam, you must understand, we cannot sustain an expense of this kind. You, who would go to Beijing and back in 24 hours to pick up a piece of paper if needed.*

There's a moment when you darken. When you talk about the will you found in the drawer on the Sunday evening they went missing. It had not been there three days earlier. Mathias must have written it and left it there before leaving. It was written in German, which was natural as it was his language. But the cops on your case were, and still are, French. They required a certified translation, it takes a week to obtain, madam. Forget that you were standing there translating it for them on the spot, yelling, read what he's written here: it says "if the girls are not present, all my worldly goods are to be left to my family," what does, "if the girls are not present," mean? They're six, why should they not be present? But the cops were not paying any attention to you. Madam, you are biased, hold your tongue. We will assign the document to a translator, trouble yourself no further. If only they had listened to you, you say. If they had grasped what was going on, as you had, they might have been able to stop him. Five days they wasted. And every day since.

*

You say about the investigation that they didn't investigate anything but your culpable decision to separate from Mathias. You go on to talk about sexism and racism. About how an Italian woman in Switzerland is totally alone in the world, and therefore a hundred times more at risk, when things get dangerous, than anywhere else. But then, no, you correct yourself: you're actually at risk wherever people around you don't see you, or don't believe you. I imagine it happens everywhere, yes. That's it, you think: it's not a self-defense manual for Switzerland that's needed, but rather a handbook on how women should make themselves heard, who women should appeal to when the country they live in doesn't have the tools—for some reason, any reason—to give them a voice. Automatic protocols should be triggered when a child goes missing. Procedures, priorities. That's why I founded Missing Children Switzerland, you say. It didn't exist before. Someone like me didn't know who to turn to in order to be heard, to get help. Now they do, you say, your whole face lighting up in a smile.

31.
CHILDREN

I don't feel any need to have more children. I've heard that when something happens to a penguin's egg, they steal another's and brood it until it hatches. I get it. Penguins are great. They're penguins, though.

You can be nostalgic about people, not categories. Your Nonna, her and her alone, not grandmothers in general. Your father, not a father. Alessia and Livia are not girls, they are Alessia and Livia. I don't miss having children: I miss them. Absence is a constant presence: it challenges you to daily hand-to-hand combat, it lays siege to you. It draws you into a fight, taking measure of your stamina. Nostalgia is physical, too. It's absolutely impossible to fill the gap left by living bodies: their smell, the softness of their skin, their voices when they call out to you. That quality of soft resistance to your embraces, that way of bending their necks. There isn't a thing, or a person, that can replace someone's absence. Only dreams. When the girls return, alive and scented, with their bodies and voices, in dreams. I'm delighted when I dream about them. I wake up overjoyed.

I enjoy children. Now that they are no longer here, I mean. I love other people's children, I have fun with them they make me laugh and I fall in love with them. I stop in the street and watch children playing. I never, and I mean never, wish they were mine. The attributes of possession should be forbidden for human beings. When I hear someone say "my wife," or "my son," I always feel uncomfortable. Mathias used to do it. There's something false and vaguely ominous in that "my." An imperceptible violence. A theft of identity. Nobody belongs to anyone, I believe. Anyone, if they wish, can belong to everybody.

There's something in me of the Irish dancer who left her children behind to emigrate to America.

There's something in me of the American mother whose daughter, Mayme, was stolen.

The distant root of a growing plant. A plant that grows inside me, my roots. My middle name is Mayme, after all.

I'm a mother and I always will be. With no children but still a mother. You don't need children to be a mother.

32.
ME ABOUT YOU. A DREAM

They came to see me last night—you say. Your eyes look bigger when they well up, they glitter in the bright light of the morning. Are you glad? I ask, stupidly. I never know how to ask you about them, I would always prefer not to. To simply imagine what you're thinking in silence. Every word can spoil, that's for sure. None of them are sufficiently accurate yet malleable, and anyway everything is so clear: clearer still without words. It's as if we'd made a pact of silence from the start. But now that it's morning—everything begins again every morning—now that you are coming into the room laden with sweets and, as you arrive you say, with your first breath: they came to see me last night, I ask you.

Overjoyed, not glad. Grateful, awestruck, and filled with joy. Because—you explain to me—it's always a little miracle and a celebration when they come to me in my dreams: they are present, they are here in my life. Dreams—you know this—are not a different place from real life: they're reality in a different form. Except there's something that doesn't make sense, how can I describe it? There's something that, when you wake up, you think: I've never seen that place, I've never owned that dress. Or just: it's impossible to breathe underwater, and yet I was breathing and talking. Do you see what I mean? Something unreal, that's what it is. Last night, though, they were real.

Real how?

They were grown up, older. They were what they're like now. Like I've never seen them. I was so moved to see them all grown up. I was overwhelmed with joy, all I could think was how beautiful they are, how different they are, but I couldn't speak. So, they came to me, into my arms.

You held them in your arms?

I wouldn't have been able to. They were grown up, I told you. And anyway, I was sitting down, in our armchair. They came to me, onto my lap, they were hugging me. So, I felt them, I held them tight and I felt their bodies. Their smell, the same but different. Their skin, less translucent but still smooth. Their ribs stronger in their chests. Their legs stretching right down to the ground, when sitting down. We hugged, we touched, we held on tight. We looked one another in the eye, laughing. I can't remember what we did then, just their eyes, looking into their eyes.

Is that how it ended, without a sound?

Without words. But there was a sound, like the sound of air. A kind of subtle vibration.

We sit in silence. I know we're both thinking about subtle vibrations. We're trying to feel them. After a while, you say, turning your head towards the window: love for your children is the only true love. And I think that kind of love, love for your children, has a sound. When you look at them and they look at you—in certain moments of silence—you can hear it. It's like a distant wave, a magnetic one. As if an invisible bow is plying the string of a viola that's not there.

No happiness can be more absolute—you seek out my eyes again, smiling at me with yours—don't you think?

33.
LET ME BE THE ONE

Let me be the one, and no one else, asking myself the questions now. Why can't I free myself from thinking about you? What is it about you that affects me so, that alters me? Why does everything seem to have settled into its place since meeting you: more difficult to define, easier to bear?

It's not the story you tell, it's not that. It's not the sequence of gestures, mysteries, details. No. I never have the slightest desire to go back over the investigation, nor do you. The facts lie outside this room, set in stone elsewhere: they are all peripheral to the matter, never central. We never ask out loud where the girls are today. There's never been the need to say it: we simply don't do it. Besides, you didn't come to find them: it would have been pointless. Not to find them, but to find someone to listen. Something about you and listening. What about me? What have I found that belongs to me but that I didn't know I was looking for?

I hardly remembered you from the newspapers. You knocked, you said: let's talk. Why? I asked. I think it'll be useful, I hope—you answered. Out of necessity. A moment later, it had become something I needed to do. Listen to you, my own need. What need, I wonder? Why?

Because everything seemed to be calm. Shipshape, just right. Everything seemed to be as it should be.

Because you were walking calmly on the edge of a precipice. Normality. One false step would have been enough. One imperceptible step sideways.

Because no, it's not true. There is a reason, right? That governs our actions. There are options, decisions. We choose who we live with, have children with, build a home with. If we can, we do.

Can we? Do we?

Tell me about your father, what he was like when you were a little girl. And now? What's he like?

Tell me again about that time when he said: you mustn't die.

Duty, duty. Don't disappoint. Be worthy. Were you a good girl? You were a good girl.

There's a tangle in the heart. There's light in the darkness. There's always shadow.

Because you need courage, you need strength. Because courage and strength are not enough.

Even if you've been a good girl, these qualities are not enough.

Tell me again about your hunches, about the coincidences.

Are we all destined to repeat other lives? Is the task we have been assigned in life to take just one step, perhaps in a circle, or maybe backwards, though it may feel like we're moving forwards?

No, it's not that exactly. You say: we can change the path of destiny, look, we can dodge it, see? We can get away from the place others have allocated to us. Other people are not our destiny. Is that what you mean? You also say: finding our place in history, that is our only task.

Because there's no such thing as time.

Because violence, love, desire, needs, silence, and words get mixed up. They blend together. Always, almost always.

Because you can live without. Seriously, you can. Live with absence. Coexist with it.

Because anything can happen to anyone. To you, to me, to anyone. Can we really not predict it, see it, know it?

Really?

Because you are kind. You're full of pain and love. Because you have a gift, a talent, for smiling.

Because you never complain. This, most of all: you never complain.

Sense and sensibility. Passion and devotion. Magic and enchantment. Doing, enduring. Loving, being loved. Guiding, letting yourself be guided.

Victims, torturers. Battles. Borders. Inside and outside, everywhere, borders.

You call them borders. There's always one side that borders on another, in life as in the binding of pages in a book.

34.
Me About You. Absence

It's only at the end of everything that I know, we both know, why this story, your story, is no ordinary story—of course it isn't—and why it's so powerful. So much so that it alters anyone who hears it. You talk about how to survive absence. How to live without the people you love more than anything else in the world. Everybody understands what this means. There's no need to imagine the experience of having your children taken away from you. Everybody knows how hard it is to coexist with, endure, and transform the absence of your loved ones. It's a never-ending occupation. A constant battle. A siege, as you call it. The presence of those who are absent besieges you.

Sometimes, you need to be able to distract yourself. It's as necessary as sleep, or water. It is essential to preserve a pristine memory of moments in the past without losing your bearings when you are there, not to live purely for those moments—in the hope, or illusion, that they will metamorphosize into the present again—and thereby stop experiencing the everyday, which is filled with other things. You push these other things out of the way, as if they were a bother. You avoid meetings, ignore looks, forget occasions. And yet, it is in these other things that life flows. You need to make peace with your destiny, whatever it is. A ball not connecting with a foot, too early, too late, too long, too little, missed *encounters, misunderstandings, I thought, but then you, how come we can't live together, why can't we, can't you see it's in the stars, can't you see it'll never be as perfect as this, between us, what's in the way, I can't believe it, I won't give up. Actually, yes, actually yes. We need to give up, you say. The only thing that's more painful than not having your loved ones near you is not knowing where your loved ones are. Not even having their bodies so that you can imagine them walking somewhere else.*

I look at you, I listen to you, and the light in everything changes. You are the rock of absence. You are its presence. Meanwhile, you smile and talk to me about love. A new love, another love. You describe it. It doesn't take anything away from the rest. On the contrary: it touches you, it holds you, it accompanies you, it takes the pack off your shoulders when it's too heavy to walk any further. It embraces you.

Searching, traveling, seeing, trying to understand what the bigger picture is. This is the only thing we can do. Not stopping ourselves, not suppressing our desire, ever. Another step. One meter further. Forgetting and remembering. Letting things out and then bringing them back into your heart.

This is what you say, before putting your things in a bag and setting off again. "Love does not forget you, even when you ignore it. It comes back and knocks. If you don't answer, it will bring you down. You need to harbor a little fear, but most of all you need to show it how brave you are. You need to be there when it calls. You need to be there and take care of it. Only when you let it go freely, will you see it return."

35.
LIST. WORDS.

Forget, remember. Etymology, root: mind, heart (OE *forgietan*: to "lose" from the mind; LT *recordari*, to record, or call something to your heart, the metaphoric seat of memory). The mind forgets. The heart does not. (*Natalia Reveulta, the woman who loved Fidel Castro before he became Fidel, when she was twenty, in the only interview she ever gave: "It took me my whole life to relocate him from my heart to my mind." Such a short journey, such a long time. And anyway, something can slip your mind. Once you've learned it by heart, though, it never will.*)

In regional or literary Italian, the words *scordare* and *rammentare* go in the opposite direction: distancing from the heart (LT: *cor, cordis*) and bringing to mind (LT: *mens, mentis*). In spoken Italian, however, it's one to a thousand: the words *ri*-cor-*dare* and *di*-men-*ti*-care win hands down. (Nonna Klara used to sing the *Recordare* from Mozart's Requiem.)

Synonyms for forget: obliterate. Oublier. Olvidar. LT *obliviscioblitum*, perhaps originally *ob* + root of *levis*, rubbed smooth, ground down. Also: discolor, efface, erase. (*Oblivion, Astor Piazzolla: music—in any case*—inolvidable, *unforgettable*.) It takes more courage to forget. To smooth things down.

(We forget four things a day, a study of the mind has revealed. The human brain wipes out four things a day— I've read—deleting them. Where do they go? Can they be recovered? How? Anyway, why four? How can they count them?)

Widower, widow: a person who has lost their spouse/companion. From Proto-Indo-European *wid-hewo*, source of the Sanskrit *vidhuh*: "lonely, solitary" and Latin *viduus*, "bereft, void," *viduare*, "deprive." Becoming empty. But also, the root *uidh-: "to separate, divide." No longer two, alone. (*A person who is one of a couple. Twins. Generated as two, born as two, brought up as two. So, if one loses the other, does that make them a twin-widow or widower?*)

Uxoricide: a man who murders a wife, *uxor*. By extension, a person who kills their spouse. A person who loses their partner by their own hand.

Orphan: a person whose parents have died. From the Greek, *orphos*, and Latin *orbus*. Bereaved, mutilated. Missing a piece. But also, deprived. In Dante, *orbati dalla luce* means deprived of light. By extension, blinded. Deprived of your orbs, or eyes. (Oublier, *going into the darkness having been deprived of your memory*.)

Patricide: a child who murders a father, by extension a parent.

Infanticide: a parent who murders a child.

The missing word.

Parents who lose children. Who don't murder them, but lose them. What are they called, how do you say it, who is someone whose child has died? What place do they occupy in history? Missing word, missing word. Missing, absent. Who eliminated it? When? From all the Italian, French, German, Spanish, English dictionaries. And why?

In German: it's missing. In French: it's missing. In Italian: it's missing. In Spanish: it's missing (*deshijado*, old-fashioned and no longer in use, indicates someone who has no children, who has not produced children). In English there's the word bereaved, deprived of someone you love. It doesn't specify who. Anyone you love.

In Hebrew it's there. It resurfaces in the Old Testament of the Bible: *av shakul* for the father, *em shakula* for the mother. Verb: *shakol* or *shakal*, to have lost your children. Genesis 27:45, Isaiah 49:21, Jeremiah 18:21. It was there then, and it's still in use in modern Hebrew.

In Arabic, there's *thaakil* for the father and *thakla* for the mother with the same root and origin as the Hebrew.

In Sanskrit, there's *vilomah*. Literally, against the natural order. The original meaning is not specific, but it is often used to signify a parent whose child has died. (*I love the word* vilomah. *I wonder whether the final h is aspirated. Like breathing. I love Sanskrit, a root and a mystery.*)

In modern Greek: *charokamenos*, burnt by Charos, or death. It is not specific, but usually refers to a parent losing a child. (*Not mutilated, as the Latin* orbos *suggests, but burnt. Not a missing piece but the whole person burned: charred in both body and soul. The whole thing. That's how it should be. It's a more precise description.*)

In ancient Greek: *orphanos*, generic, indicates both bereavements. Of those who have lost their parents and those who have lost their children. Absence in both directions. An identical absence. (*But it's not the same. It's not the same. Why isn't there a word to express Andromache's anguish when her son Astyanax was thrown to his death from the walls of Troy? Is the death of your aging mother the same as that of your newborn baby?*)

Orphanios, with an *i*. A unique case. An epigram in the *Greek Anthology*, Book VII (Tomb Epigrams), Fragment 466: Leonidas. A mother on her son's tomb, "Oh unhappy Anticles, and I most unhappy who have laid on the pyre my only son in the bloom of his youth! At eighteen you did perish, my child, and I weep and bewail my old age bereft of you."[1] There the word is with an *i*. Poetic license, the annotation indicates. (*Only poetry can see what others can't, don't know how to, or don't want to see. Poetry is music.*)

Teknoleteira. In Sophocles' *Electra*, 108. Antigone is addressing a nightingale that has lost its chick. (*Music, the song of a nightingale.*) Root: *teknon*, child, and *ollumni*, to lose something, but also to kill. The word was used only once and researchers have pointed out its controversial message. As Electra grieves for her father, Agamemnon, she compares herself to a nightingale: "Like the nightingale, slayer of her offspring, I will wail without ceasing, and cry aloud to all here at the doors of my father."[2] This is a reference to Procne, daughter of the Athenian king Pandion, who is transformed into a nightingale as punishment for killing her son and serving him up to her husband. (*Niobe, Tantalus's daughter, the archetype of a*

---

[1] A.S.F. Gow & D.L. Page, *The Greek Anthology: Hellenistic Epigrams*.
[2] Sophocles. *The Electra of Sophocles*, edited with introduction and notes by Sir Richard Jebb, Cambridge University Press, 1894.

bereaved mother, whose seven sons Artemis kills, is turned into a rock, which continues to weep when the snow melts. In some versions into a nightingale. A singing rock. A song that humans can't hear. Underwater singing. The singing of whales. My voice and theirs, in secret. Just for us.

36.
ME ABOUT YOU. OUR PLACE

Help me say what can't be said, you ask me.
This would be the most extraordinary outcome.
Managing to say out loud, dry-eyed, the things that can't be said because no one knows where to put them, no one wants to hold them, because they burn. And you—when people ask about you—feel guilty because you are a red-hot ember that scorches anyone that touches it. People ask: Do you have children? You say nothing. Yes, two, you'd like to say. Because it's true, you have two. They're there all the time. You can't free yourself of their absence. Of their presence, yes, you can forget for a moment. You're in another room, focusing on a job, you're distracted by something else and you're not thinking about them: you know that their presence can flit in and out, it'll be back with one gesture, that part is easy. It's their absence you can never forget. It doesn't allow you any distraction, ever. So, you end up saying: yes, I have two. Then you should add: but they're dead. Presumed dead, if you really want to be precise. But you don't say it. You don't say it spontaneously and then it's too late, and you can't find the courage to say it. Courage, yes, that's the word. Because you're ashamed to embarrass people. Do you see what I'm saying? You know that once you've said it, the response from that moment on and forever after will be a sentiment of horror, pity, and denial, feelings that

weren't there until a second before—in their smiles and in their polite conversation—and a second later can never be eradicated. They truly didn't want to know: they didn't want to hear it. It's a marginal system error—you say, surprisingly retrieving the jargon of a businesswoman as your hands dig deeper into the black box of your soul—since feeling guilty for embarrassing a stranger you speak to on the train is minimum collateral damage. Minimum and collateral, you mean, compared to absolute pain. Because this, too, must be said— can I light a cigarette, do you mind? Shall I open a window?—it must be said that losing a child is the touchstone of grief, the gold standard of pain. The benchmark. Every other difficulty in life—sickness, acute physical pain, abandonment, extreme poverty—is contained within its perimeter. It puts things into perspective, in a certain sense, recognizing the borders, knowing the confines of pain. I know, I know, it sounds sacrilegious to say that knowing the confines of pain is a privilege. And yet, it's true. In your life afterwards, it's true. I read a book once called Portraits of a Marriage *by Sándor Márai.[3] One of the characters is talking about this and that and says to another, speaking of himself: you don't know, I can see by the way you're looking at me, you don't know what I'm talking about and I pity you. That's more or less how I remember it. I remember the verb: pity. To feel bad for someone who doesn't know. The privilege of knowing. At a price, of course. But something that is truly invaluable— knowledge, for example, but profound love, too—always has a price, doesn't it?*

[3] *Portraits of a Marriage* by Sándor Márai, tr. George Szirtes, Vintage, 2012.

Well, do you know what would be amazing? If people you speak to about yourself had the capacity to hold their peace, listen, and not feel duty-bound to put their two cents of horrified clichés in. To accept, and find a place for what you're saying. At the end of the day, it's not so unusual, you know? There are thousands of people every day who lose a child. Accidents disease drugs war violence madness. Every minute. That's why I wonder why our language has abolished the word for expressing it. You're a widow if you lose your husband. You're an orphan if you lose one parent or both. But what am I? What are we? You'll say: why does having a word matter to you? It matters. Because having a name means having a place, a home, made up of thoughts that have already been thought. A warm place where thousands, millions of people have been before you. It makes you feel, despite the error, like you're in the right place. A place that is painful and illuminating, a place that is hard but intended as part of the history of the world.

Now, let's go for a stroll, shall we? Let's go outside and see, because it looks like Spring has come.

Concita and Irina would be overjoyed if this book contributed to supporting and sustaining at length the invaluable work of Missing Children Switzerland.

www.missingchildren.ch

ABOUT THE AUTHOR

Concita De Gregorio is a writer, journalist, and broadcaster. One of *la Repubblica*'s best-known and long-established columnists, she has written several works of non-fiction on politics, current affairs, and issues concerning women and children. She was the Editor of *l'Unità* newspaper, and is the creator and host of several successful news and current affairs programs for Italian national radio and television. *The Missing Word* is her second novel.